THE
BOATHOUSE

Kintsukuroi: The art of mending broken pots with gold

DOUGLAS MURRAY

malcolm down

PUBLISHING

First published 2021 by Malcolm Down Publishing Ltd.
www.malcolmdown.co.uk

24 23 22 21   7 6 5 4 3 2 1

British Library Cataloguing in Publication Data
A catalogue record for this book is available from the British Library.

ISBN 978-1-912863-84-6

Cover design by Esther Kotecha
Art direction by Sarah Grace

Printed in the UK

AUTHOR'S NOTE

The Boathouse is a story about the healing power of writing and our human need to leave something behind to show that our life had meaning, or in Japanese our ikigai, our reason for living.

The novel is in three parts as the three main protagonists take it in turns to describe their life in an old boathouse on the west coast of Hokkaido. A wandering beggar, a young fisherwoman, and an old poet, united in their experience of the healing power of telling the story of their time in the boathouse.

Three lives, three pebbles dropped into the sea, the ripples converging into transient patterns of interconnection as they each try to come to terms with their fragility and search for meaning. This search ultimately leads them all back to the boathouse, to rediscover the profound impact it had upon their lives.

Douglas Murray.

PROLOGUE

The boathouse sits on the shore of a small inlet on the west coast of Hokkaido. Its oak timbers, seasoned by the passing years, are now beginning to show signs of neglect. Cracks and crevices within the grey floorboards, which no longer quite meet, creak in protest against any footfall.

Sitting on the porch, which doubles as a makeshift jetty, an old man gazes out to sea. An ancient fishing boat he is no longer able to sail creaks with every pull of the tide against the rope holding it captive to its ramshackle mooring.

Turning his eyes to the tattered yellow sail, the old man remembers taking the boat out in his youth and returning at sunset, his young wife waiting on the jetty to help him land his catch. All gone now, washed away by time and tide, like pebbles on a beach taken away by the waves.

The old man reaches into his pocket and takes out a weathered notebook in which he writes down his poems and reflections, all that will remain when time and tide wash him away also. As he opens the book, a yellowing piece of rice paper falls to the floor of the jetty and with a sigh the old man bends down and saves it with trembling hands just before it falls into the sea.

The old man gently unfolds the paper and peers at the words, although he knows them by heart. A haiku, written by a young poet named Ame.

Pebbles on a beach
glistening in the sunlight
waiting for the waves.

'In haiku we see the world as a single pebble, and the tears of the world in every drop of rain.' The old man smiles as he remembers saying this to the young poet, whom he had met by chance on the beach, and how that chance meeting had changed his life forever.

With the poem still in his hands, the old man once again gazes out to sea, watching as the sunset turns the Sea of Japan translucent, with the dying light shimmering on the water with all the transient impermanence of life.

The old man smiles again as a poem starts to take shape in his mind. Reaching for his pen, he starts to capture the moment in haiku. It is the old poet's ikigai, his reason for living, to capture such moments of transient beauty for eternity. He hopes that when he is gone, whoever moves into the boathouse will perhaps find his book of poems, his life's work, his life's love, his writing.

BOOK ONE

1

Bathed in blue moonlight
reflections of the boathouse
fishing boats at rest.

Ame

My feet sink into the soft snow as I make my way through the wood in the stillness of winter, a frosty moon casting blue shadows all around me. My breath rises into the freezing air as I pull the collar of my coat further up around my ears to try and keep warm. So very cold and tired now, I know I must find shelter soon.

I can feel my body starting to shut down minute by minute, the cold creeping deeper into my bones like some malignant force. An all-pervading tiredness overwhelms me, which I know will kill me if I give in to it and lay down in the snow.

From behind me, somewhere in the shadows, the terrifying howl of a wolf breaks the silence of the night. I hurl myself forward in sheer panic, but my strength is all but gone and I fall flat on my face. Is this how it all ends?

When I turn around, there is no sign of my stalker, but every instinct tells me that it is out there lurking in the shadows, waiting for its moment. From somewhere inside, an instinct for survival gives me the strength to struggle to my feet and carry on, but it is short lived and I know that I can not go on much longer.

Then, through the freezing mist I see the outline of an old hut, half buried in the snow. As I draw nearer I can begin to make out the heavy oak beams of its rugged construction, built to withstand the severe Hokkaido winters. The heavy oak door is frosted over, but sheer desperation gives me the strength to force the latch up and slide the door open enough for me to slip inside.

Falling to my knees with exhaustion, I take in my surroundings. A pale shaft of moonlight falling through a small dusty window shows the hut to be completely empty apart from a small wooden satsuru. I find myself wondering who last sat upon it and how long ago? A feeling of timelessness lingers in the air, an oasis of stillness, a place where one might seek solitude or refuge from the world outside. With this in mind I quickly turn around and secure the rough wooden latch, remembering the danger that stalked my steps through the snow.

Surrendering to my feelings of total exhaustion, I curl up in the corner on the bare wooden floor. As I wait for sleep to overtake me, the smell of the oak timbers reminds me of the old boathouse and my life there, on the west coast of Hokkaido with my mother Taki-san. The boathouse had been in our family for years, with each generation leaving their mark in the form of repairs and patches to the oak timbers. At night as I lay on my tatami, I would fall asleep to the sound of our old boat rocking back and forth against the porch.

I do not know how long I slept, but the cold awakens me to the grim reality of my rough shelter in the woods. Rubbing the cold from my bones, I stand up and stretch, my hands touching the beams of the roof. I realise that I must make the most of my good fortune in finding this refuge and spend the night here, before trying to make my way north again in the morning. Wolves tend to stalk their prey at night and I have no intention of venturing out until daylight, even if I had the strength to do so, which I do not. I am very aware that if I had not found this old hut then I would have died out there tonight, and all my travels through

Japan and all my searching for my ikigai, my reason for living, would have come to a sudden end.

Through the small dusty window, I can just make out the silvery white trunks of a small clump of kabanoki trees, casting their shadows on the snow. Then I hear the distinctive sound of a flock of whooper swans heading south. Looking up, I catch a fleeting glimpse of their snow-white wings fading into the frosty mist on their migration from the harsh Hokkaido winter, their plaintiff call like a warning for others to flee from the cold.

As a boy I would sit by the window of the boathouse gazing into the sky, waiting to see the first whooper swans coming to land in our bay to rest on their southern migration. I would sit for hours on our porch, watching and listening to them calling to each other in the frozen mist. I still have my drawings of them, the rice paper now yellow with age somehow making the white swans appear golden and even more mystical.

The swans would stay only for a few days until suddenly the whole flock would race across the bay and take to the air again in a flurry of snow-white wings. I would sit there until the last little speck of white faded over the horizon, leaving me alone again, then Taki–san would come and sit beside me on the porch with her arm around my shoulder. She knew when not to say anything that might break the poignant silence of the passing of the swans.

Taki-san was often silent, her beautiful dark eyes growing thoughtful as she became lost in her inner world. Then it would be my turn to know not to say anything to break her inmost thoughts. We lived alone in the boathouse, making our living by catching fish from the old boat. The boat was like an extension of the boathouse, as it too had been patched up over the years by our family, of whom I am now the last.

Before I was born, Taki-san had lived with her grandfather, and it was he who had taught her how to fish, both her parents having died when

9

she was an infant. When her grandfather died, she was left alone in the boathouse, until she fell in love with my father Shusaku-san, but when he died at sea, she was left alone again until I was born. And so, silence became part of Taki-san's world; we could go for hours in our fishing boat without saying a word, just listening to the sound of the sea until it was time to pull in the nets and head back to the boathouse for the evening.

Taki-san died while she was still very young. Perhaps it was the hard life she had to live, looking after me and doing everything for us. I was born too early and was crippled from birth, so I could do little to help her.

Our old priest Fr. Koji conducted a most beautiful funeral service for Taki-san in our little church on the hill, which overlooks the sea. Sadly I was the only person there. We had been shunned all our lives by the people in the fishing village, and now even at her death they had all kept their distance.

'Try to forgive them, Ame-san,' the old priest said as we carried my mother's ashes back to the boathouse. 'They are a simple and superstitious people.'

'I don't think Taki-san would have wanted them to attend anyway father,' I replied. 'Her funeral service was beautiful just as it was. Domo origato father.'

'Well said, Ame-san,' said the old priest. 'Your mother led a beautifully simple life with just the two of you. Your presence here was all that she would have wanted.'

When we arrived at the boathouse, Fr. Koji stepped into the boat and steadied it for me to get aboard with the little pot of Taki-san's ashes. Then, when I was seated in the stern, he cast off and unfurled the sail to take us out to sea. Our destination, the two rocks just a little offshore, was very special to Taki-san and I knew that she would want to be buried there.

When we arrived at our destination, Fr. Koji brought the boat alongside and tied it to the rocks, just as I had watched Taki-san do on many occasions.

'We used to come out here every year father,' I said. 'On the anniversary of my father's death.'

'I knew Shusaku-san very well,' replied the old priest. 'A terrible tragedy, Ame-san, to die so young, trying to save the life of another fisherman. Your father was a very brave man.'

'I am just so sorry that I never knew him,' I replied. 'But Taki-san never tired of telling me about him.'

'And now they will be united again,' said the old priest. 'And it is your turn now to be brave, Ame-san. Your life will not be easy, I'm afraid.'

'I know that, father. Taki-san told me one day that I must find my own ikigai, and that we all have our own unique reason for living. I have not found it yet, but in honour of my mother, that is what I now intend to do.'

'Then God bless you, Ame-san, and help you to find it.'

The old priest and I then lapsed into a moment of silence as we listened to the sound of the water lapping against the side of the boat.

'And now let us lay Taki-san to rest,' he said. 'In this very special place that was so dear to her heart.'

The old priest then said a most beautiful prayer for Taki-san's soul, that it would sail safely to that distant shore beyond the sea, where Shusaku-san awaited her.

Following Fr. Koji's instructions, I reached over the side and held the little pot of Taki-san's ashes in the water for a moment. Then I opened my fingers and let it sink into the deep, as the setting sun turned the sea and the sky into liquid gold.

We cast off from the rocks and sailed back to the boathouse in silence, lost in our own thoughts about the very special person to whom we had now said our final sayonara. I thanked Fr. Koji once again as he took his leave, then went back inside the boathouse to be alone with my memories of our solitary lives in this old place.

The boathouse sits on the shore of an isolated little bay on the very edge of our fishing village, so there was always distance between us and the rest of the fishing community. Fishermen put their lives at the mercy of the sea every time they set out, so they are superstitious by nature, observing rituals and looking for signs of good or bad omens. The sea is our mother and feeds us, but she can often turn cruel and take our lives.

My mother suffered a lot of sadness in her life, with her parents dying when she was an infant, then her grandfather dying in the boat with her at the helm. Then, when her fiancé died at sea, a cruel rumour was started among the fishermen that Taki-san was un no waru, unlucky. So the villagers started to avoid us and we had to live our lives with little or no contact with them.

With Taki-san now gone, I was left completely on my own. I have never been strong enough to sail our boat, so I had no way to earn a living. I was left with no choice but to start to beg. This proved impossible, as the people of the village continued to shun me and look away as I sat by the roadside with my begging bowl. It was as though they now looked upon me as the source of the bad luck and would cross the road to avoid me. Eventually I had no choice but to leave the boathouse and walk to the next village to beg there.

The people in the next village were kinder at first and would put coins or food in my begging bowl, but after a while they grew tired of me and stopped giving me anything. And so I became a kojiki, a wandering beggar, constantly moving from village to village.

Sometimes people are kind and sometimes they are cruel. Sometimes the children would come and dance around me, laughing and calling me waretta, broken, because of my crippled legs. At first this made me feel ashamed, but I have learned to ignore it; they are only children and do not realise how words can be cruel and hurtful.

The silence now descends upon the old hut once again as the last of the whooper swans call fades away into the night. Looking once again at the kabanoki trees, I notice how the wind has peeled strips off their silvery white bark, making them look like little scraps of rice paper flapping in the breeze. They remind me of my collection of haiku written on old scraps of paper, which I find just lying around, waiting for me to transform them into works of art.

Taki-san was a beautiful haiku poet, and I would listen to her words with delight as we sat in the boathouse in the long winter evenings, burning the driftwood we collected on the shore in our little black pot-bellied stove. I never wrote haiku at that time, as my love was to draw haikai pictures of the swans and the boat, but I loved to listen to her very soft and gentle voice reading what she had written that day out on the water as we waited for the fish to fill our net.

It was always Taki-san's wish that I too would write haiku, but for some reason I never felt the need to express my feelings in writing. All that was to change when I had to leave the boathouse and take to the road.

One day, when I was begging by the roadside, a most beautiful geisha came walking toward me. With the morning sun behind her and shining through her yellow kimono, she looked ten kara no, heavenly. I must have been staring at her because she stopped and smiled, then in the most beautiful voice, she said, 'Ohayo-gozaimasu.'

I was so amazed she had said good morning to me that I just stared at her, completely lost for words. Then she gave a delightful little laugh, bowed and then walked away, her yellow silk kimono flowing in the air like the wings of a butterfly.

Taki-san had taught me that the aim of haiku was to capture fleeting moments of outstanding beauty and that one day, when I had such an experience, then hopefully I too would begin to write haiku. I had now experienced such a haiku moment, and in it I was changed from being a wandering beggar into a wandering haiku poet. While words like waretta, broken, can be ugly and hurtful, as a haiku poet I now use words to create beauty and solace.

Sitting down on the little satsuru in the corner of the old hut, I reach into my pockets and search through my ragged collection of haiku until I find my very first one, now yellowing with age, about my encounter with the beautiful geisha.

Wandering beggar
following a butterfly
dancing on the air.

I never saw her again, and she will never know how by simply saying good morning to me she changed my life forever. Having experienced the transforming power of words, as a haiku poet I am now very aware of the healing power of writing, for it touches something at the core of our being. If written well, it can also touch and heal the wounds in those who read it, like one soul reaching out to another.

With a final look at my very first haiku, I very carefully roll it up again and put it back with the rest of my treasured collection. Little three-line poems written on worthless scraps of paper, but to me they are priceless memories of my travels all around the coast of Japan, a journey which has now led me here to this old hut in the woods, where I must spend the night.

2

Softly in the night
moonlit shadows in the snow
while the beggar sleeps.

Ame

Sitting in the dark in this old hut stirs so many memories. Once again I am reminded of the last time that I saw the boathouse, its wooden beams all covered with snow, as I left to start my journey as a wandering beggar. It was like leaving a part of me behind, the best part that I had spent with Taki-san.

As I followed the coastal path, I turned to take one final look, not knowing when, or if, I would ever see it again. I had lost Taki-san, and now I was losing that very special place where we had known such happiness together. It felt as though something inside of me was being torn away and left to die with every step I took.

As time went by, however, I began to take solace in discovering that all the beautiful memories of our time together in the boathouse were still very much alive in my heart. It was these memories that kept me going in those very hard early days as a wandering beggar. At night, as I huddled in some corner from the cold, I had only to close my eyes and I would be back in the boathouse sleeping on my tatami and listening to Taki-san's breath, in time with the tide rocking against our old boat.

Because of the weakness of my legs I can only walk slowly and it can take over a day for me to cover the distance between villages, but the coastal paths which I take are a constant source of inspiration for my haiku and the time does not seem long. At night when I find a place to sleep, I reflect on my day's journey, sometimes turning my reflections into a haiku on one of my pieces of old scrap paper.

One evening when I was sitting by the sea and writing a haiku, I became aware that I was being watched by an elderly man with long white hair and a little wispy beard. When he saw that I was aware of him, he came over and sat beside me.

'Haiku?' he asked, looking down at my scrap of paper.

'It's about how the setting sun glistens on the wet pebbles as the tide flows over them,' I replied.

'May I look?' asked the old man.

I rather shyly handed him my dirty piece of rice paper, then watched as he read it slowly in a quiet, reflective sort of way. He struck me as being rather scholarly, perhaps even aesthetic in his manner.

'This is good,' he said, handing the haiku back to me. 'You have captured the moment well.'

This was the first time that anyone had ever read one of my haiku and I was pleased that this scholarly old man had thought it was good. I thanked him and explained that I had only recently taken up haiku.

'Then you show promise as a beginner,' he replied. 'You must keep it up. I myself attempt to write one haiku each day.'

This was very encouraging, that a real haiku poet felt that I had promise. We talked a little about haiku, then a natural silence fell between us as we sat there watching the sea. After a while, he turned to me and asked if he could see my haiku again.

'Of course,' I replied, only too eager for him to look at it again.

To my surprise the old man then turned my haiku over and began to write on the reverse of the rice paper. While I had pondered long and hard to construct my haiku, his appeared to flow effortlessly with hardly a pause between the three lines. When he was finished, he sat in silence looking at his work for a moment, then handed it back to me.

'My haiku for the day,' he said. 'Please accept it as my gift to you, and your first lesson in haiku.'

A lesson which I will never forget, for his haiku was indeed a work of art, about how each pebble was unique and how they all become beautifully polished by being washed around on the shore, until the sea came in once again to carry them back into the deep.

It struck me that he had taken my simple haiku theme to a greater depth of beauty and meaning, with the pebbles becoming a metaphor for those who lived out their hard lives by the sea. When I told him this, he looked steadily at me for a moment.

'In haiku we see the world in a single pebble,' he said, 'and the tears of the world in every drop of rain. So you see, my young haiku poet, your third line about waiting for waves to make the pebbles glisten is beautiful, but it also contains the deeper meaning about carrying them back out to sea. And then we see the world in your pebbles, and its tears in the waves.'

The old poet then said something quite strange as we stood up to say goodbye.

'We have shared a haiku moment and I recognise a kindred spirit, but for the soul of a haiku poet to blossom, it must look upon Fuji-san. Sayonara, my young haiku poet.'

As I watched him walk away along the beach, he seemed totally at one with the elements, his footsteps light and unhurried. I found myself wishing that one day I too could become like him, elemental, absorbing the natural world around him, and transforming it into haiku with such effortless grace.

I watched the last rays of the sun going down into the sea, then made my own way along the coast again until I found a place which offered a bit of shelter for the night. As I lay there watching the moon and waiting for sleep to overtake me, I pondered on the old poet's parting words, that for the soul of the haiku poet to blossom, it must look upon Fuji-san. But what little hope had I of ever making such a journey to Japan's most holy mountain in the south of Honshu? Such a thing was of course impossible for a crippled beggar to contemplate. However, the old poet had sown a seed of inspiration in my heart and when sleep finally overtook me I dreamed of sitting on the slopes of Mount Fujiyama and writing my haiku.

I awoke the next day with the dream still very much in my mind and as I took to the road to make my way toward the next village to beg, I began to ask myself if such a journey could indeed be possible. When I had initially took to the road after leaving the boathouse, I had headed north, possibly for no better reason than that was the direction the whooper swans had taken in the early spring.

As the time went by, I had continued to simply follow the coastline up and around Hokkaido. I was now making my way south down the east coast of the island. The thought now struck me that rather than walking aimlessly in circles, I could now begin to walk with a purpose, my goal being to see Fuji-san.

Of course, such a journey would take a very long time, but one thing beggars have plenty of is time. And what was I doing with all this time I had? Merely existing from one begging bowl to the next. In that moment it struck me that time was the greatest of all treasures and that I should spend it on a more noble cause.

So I determined on that day to live my life like an adventure, rather than an existence. A wise man once said that a journey of a thousand miles begins with the first step, and so with a smile on my face I stretched out my foot and took my first step toward the most beautiful place in all Japan, to see Mount Fujiyama, the holy mountain.

As I look out of the small window in the old hut, I notice a gentle fall of snow from one of the branches of the kabanoki trees. I have always loved snow; it is like a pure gift falling down from heaven in perfect silence. It also has a very practical application for thirsty beggars. I very cautiously unlatch the door again and slide it open to peer outside, very aware of the danger that had followed in my footsteps to the hut.

All is still and quiet, but around the door of the hut there are clear wolf tracks in the snow. I shudder as I imagine it following my own tracks to the hut and then lurking there in the night while I slept. With my eyes still on the shadows of the woods, I reach down and scoop up some snow in my begging bowl, a trick I learned to quench my thirst. As I do so, my hand touches something hard and cold. Scooping the snow away, I find an old broken pot that has been cast aside, too badly broken to be of any use. But to a haiku poet a broken pot can be just as much of a hidden treasure as a scrap of rice paper.

Something about this small broken pot lying in the snow touches my heart and so I pick it up and carry it inside the hut with me. Then I slide the door closed again and taste some of the snow. Curling up on the floor in the corner of the hut with the broken pot beside me, a haiku slowly begins to take shape in my mind as I wait for the stillness of the woods to take me to sleep.

<blockquote>
Lying in the snow
in the stillness of the woods
an old broken pot.
</blockquote>

I smile as the old poet's words drift back to my mind about seeing the world in a single pebble. I wonder, what he would see in an old broken pot? I owe that old poet a great debt of gratitude, not only for opening my mind to the depths that lay hidden in the apparent simplicity of the three lines of haiku, but for inspiring me to set out on a journey which deepened my experience of life.

As my own haiku deepened with time, I began also to reflect upon the old poet's teaching that in haiku we see the tears of the world in every drop of rain. But while haiku can present the poignant beauty and sadness of life, it cannot give the answer as to why life is like this. Perhaps my ikigai, my reason for living that I am still searching for, is to find the answer.

3

On a frosted branch
an owl hooting at the moon
as the forest sleeps.

Ame

S omething in the night awakens me. In the faint grey light from
the dusty window, I strain my ears to listen. For homeless beggars
there is always danger in sleep, when we are at our most vulnerable.
I find myself thinking again about the wolf following my scent in the
snow to the door of the hut. Then the stillness of the night is broken
again, by nothing more threatening than the hooting of a night owl from
the branches of the kabanoki trees outside the window; another solitary
creature like me, alone in the night.

I smile at my timidity and then, drinking the last of the melted snow
in my bowl, I turn onto my side and try to go back to sleep. With the
taste of this pure Hokkaido water still in my mouth, my mind drifts back
to the boathouse and the old oak barrel at the corner which caught the
rain as it fell from our roof. Being as old as the rest of the house, it had
developed a few cracks over the years, which allowed the water to leak
out a little. As a child I would run my fingers over the damp patches and
taste the rain, now tinged with the taste of ancient oak.

On rainy days I would delight in sitting on the porch just listening to
the rain falling on our roof and making its way down into the barrel. On
one of these occasions Taki-san came over and sat close to me with her
arm around me and we listened to the rain together.

'Would you like me to tell you a secret, raindrop?' she asked.

This was her special name for me sometimes, as my real name is Ame, which means rain.

'A secret?'

'The secret about your name,' she said.

Taki-san then went on to tell me how she had felt so terribly lonely after my father had died that she had wanted to walk into the sea to be with him. But then one night, as she lay in the darkness listening to the rain falling onto the roof of our old boathouse, she felt my heartbeat within her, and knew she was no longer alone. And so she had named me Ame, because I had come to her in the rain.

'So you see,' Taki-san said, 'why I called you Ame, and why we both love listening to the rain.'

We sat there for a long moment listening to the rain. Then I held her hand.

'What is it, Ame-san?' she asked, turning to look into my eyes. She knew me so well that she could even read the slightest touch of my hand.

'The other children call me waretta,' I replied. 'Why am I broken, Taki-san?'

She looked at me for a long moment and I will never forget the depth of sadness in those beautiful eyes. Then she held me very close for a long time and I could feel that she was crying.

'You were born too soon, Ame-san,' she said finally. 'After your father died, I became very ill and was not strong enough to carry you inside me for very long. You were very small when you were born. Your legs have remained very weak and that is why you find it hard to walk. But you have a special beauty inside you Ame-san, which none of the other children have.'

'What is that?' I asked.

'That is the secret which only you can answer, Ame-san. It is said that God has hidden a secret within everything that he has made, and that it is for us to find it. To find our own ikigai, our reason for being alive.'

'And have you found your ikigai Taki-san?' I asked.

At this she held me very close once again and then whispered into my ear, 'You, Ame-san. You are my ikigai.'

As the years went by, Taki-san and I spent many other days sitting close together on our porch and listening to the rain. However, I have yet to find that special secret which Taki-san said is hidden within me. While over the years my love for haiku has enriched my life, there are countless haiku poets in Japan, so there is nothing special about that. So the question remains, what is my special reason for living? What is my ikigai?

Speaking of special secrets, some days when we were fortunate enough to catch all the fish we needed early, we would sail our boat to our own little secret cove and spend the rest of the day there. It was perfectly secluded and you could only get to it by sea. It was quite small, with a sandy beach surrounded by small cliffs where a little waterfall flowed out from the rock face. The water was always perfectly cold even on sunny days and we would drink our fill and wash our face, with Taki-san splashing me with it and laughing.

I miss her so very much and now understand why she had felt so alone that she wanted to walk into the sea to be with my father. But I have all these beautiful memories of our time together, and they keep her alive in my heart. Perhaps it is because we had always lived solitary lives that I can cope with being alone now. For a haiku poet, however, solitude can have its own secret blessings. In solitude one has the time and the silence to contemplate upon things that other people may not notice, and perhaps try to find the secrets hidden within them. To a haiku poet even the sound of raindrops falling into an old water barrel can be a hidden treasure.

With all these memories running through my mind, I find it hard to get back to sleep. Searching through my pockets, I take out another of my little worthless treasures, a cheap little red glass akari. When I left the boathouse to take to the road, all I took with me was my bowl to beg with and this little akari. It belonged to Taki-san and each night when we lit the candle inside it, our room would be filled with its soft red light. It was my way of taking something of Taki-san with me on the road.

In the silence of the night, I light a piece of candle, put it in my akari lamp and imagine that I am once again back in the boathouse with Taki-san sleeping gently on the floor beside me on her tatami, listening to her quiet breathing as the wind outside rocks our boat against its moorings.

On my travels I keep a look out for old pieces of candle which people throw away. When I light them and put them into the akari, I imagine what secrets might be hidden inside the candles about the people who lit them before me. At night I often watch all the lights burning in the windows of the village I happen to be passing through. Then as the lights go out one by one as the village settles down for the night, my mind drifts back to the boathouse and how Taki-san and I used to do the same.

As Taki-san's life drew to a close, I sat beside her as she rested upon her tatami by the window, listening to the swans calling to each other out in the bay, shrouded by a fine sea-mist. She caught me gazing out of the window and smiled.

'Sit out there on the porch for a moment,' she said. 'Tell me what it looks like.'

'I'd rather stay here with you,' I replied.

'I want you to,' she insisted, gently touching my face. 'Then tell me what it's like, in a haiku.'

I smiled at her, for she was always trying to make a haiku poet out of me. But I did what I was told and sat outside on the porch, listening to the swans calling to each other in the mist. I was out there for an hour or so, but never did get around to writing her haiku. When I went back inside she had fallen asleep with her book of haiku still in her hands, but when I tried to take the book from her hand I realised that she had gone.

She still had her pen in her hand and as I let my tears fall, I opened her book and read her last ever haiku, knowing that it was her parting gift to me. It was about listening to the sound of the swans in the mist, like voices drifting out to sea. It was the haiku she had asked me to write, knowing that I never would.

When I left the boathouse to take to the road, I was tempted to tear her last haiku out and carry it with me, but it felt wrong to tear it away from all her other ones. So I put her haiku book back into the drawer of her tebaru by the window, her special place where she had written them.

4

Sailing in moonlight
across an ocean of stars
the soul of haiku.

Ame

When Taki-san died, I lit our akari and prayed that her soul would fly straight to heaven to be with my father Shusaku-san. My father was lost at sea before I was born, and every year on the anniversary of his death Taki-san and I would take our boat out to their special place, where the two rocks jut out from the sea. The rocks are bound together with a thick rope. In Japan this is done to symbolise how two natural objects appear in such harmony that their tamashi, their spirit, are bound together, sharing one destiny.

Taki-san told me that she and my father would often meet in secret out there and tie their boats together like the two rocks, binding their tamashi together. So every year on the anniversary of his death we would tie our boat to the rocks then light our akari and pray for his soul.

Once a year in our village, the fishermen hold a traditional Shinto ceremony which involves making paper boats and setting them out to sea with little lamps in them, to remember the fishermen that were lost at sea and to pray for good fortune in the coming year. So every year I keep this ceremony privately wherever I am, and set out a little paper boat with a candle in it for Taki-san and Shusaku-san.

My eyes now rest on my little akari lamp casting its small circle of light in the old hut. It has been my sole companion in all my travels, my comfort in the cold and my friend in loneliness. Can a cheap little glass lamp have a tamashi, a spirit? Who knows, but over the years we have grown very close and to me it is priceless, like a little silent haiku.

As a wandering beggar I may therefore appear to have nothing, but I have all these little priceless treasures to keep me company. I also have my priceless memories of my life with Taki-san in our wonderful old boathouse on the edge of that beautiful bay on the west coast of Hokkaido. While some memories tend to fade over time, those closest to my heart simply grow deeper and richer with the passing years.

And so, as I curl up on the floor of this old hut and wait for sleep to wash over me once again, I let my eyes rest upon the light from my akari and let my mind drift back to the boathouse where I spent so many beautiful nights and where Taki-san sleeps in our moonlit bay. I remember one night as we sat on the porch of the boathouse looking at the moon on the water. Taki-san put her arm around me and whispered one of her haiku into my ear.

From an old boathouse
watching moonlight on the sea
stillness of the night.

I smile as I think how happy Taki-san must now be that she has finally got her wish for me to become a haiku poet. As I lay here in the night, the words of the old haiku poet come to mind, 'For the soul of the haiku poet to blossom, it must look upon Fuji-san.' The first part of my journey to the holy mountain took me all the way down the east coast of Hokkaido. My way of life remained the same, staying in a village until the people got tired of my begging, and then moving on once again, always south in the direction of Mount Fuji.

When I finally reached the southern tip of Hokkaido, I sat on the shore to contemplate how I could now overcome the little matter of the

Sea of Japan to continue my journey down through the main island of Honshu. Begging for food was difficult enough, but begging for a ferry ticket was verging on the impossible. Day after day I sat by the harbour wall and while people did drop food and small coins into my begging bowl, I began to accept the possibility that this may be as far as I was ever going to get to Fuji-san.

Then one day, as I sat there in the rain, I took out one of my haikai drawings of the whooper swans to cheer myself up. As I looked at the drawing, a haiku came to mind about swans flying through the rain.

Through the mist and rain
the call of swans flying south
white wings in the clouds.

With nothing else to write upon, I simply wrote the haiku on the haikai drawing. Then as I watched, the rain drops that fell on the rice paper began to merge the words into the ink drawing of the flying swans. As I sat there looking at this beautiful thing, I became aware of a little boy who had wandered over to look at me and was now staring down at my haiku.

His mother came rushing over and took his hand to lead him away, but then she stopped and also began to take an interest in what I had done. After a moment, she smiled at me and dropped a large coin into my bowl then bowed and went away.

In a moment of inspiration I turned my haiku outward, to let passers by see it. Japanese people love haiku. What I did not know at that time is that when you combine a haiku with a traditional haikai drawing it becomes a haiga, a much higher form of art which is even more deeply loved.

Within minutes more people began to stop and look at my work and drop more money into my bowl. By the end of the day I had made enough to buy my ferry ticket and stood at the rear of the boat watching Hokkaido shrink away into the distance. My haiga had overcome the obstacle of the Sea of Japan and I was once again on my way to the holy mountain.

It was dark when the ferry sailed into Honshu harbour, with a persistent rain promising me an uncomfortable night if I could not find shelter. As I made my way ashore I noticed a few unsavoury looking characters hanging around the docks and paying me an uncomfortable amount of interest.

As a homeless beggar I have developed a keen sense of danger, and this prompted me to get far away from them as quickly as my poor legs could take me. I resisted the temptation to look back to see if I was being followed, as experience had taught me that this makes me look even more like a potential victim. Turning a corner, I noticed a stack of old wooden crates and quickly took refuge in these in the hope that if I was followed, my pursuers would pass on by and not think of looking for me there.

The crates had a strong smell of fish as I buried myself deep into the back of them and lay very still. Shortly afterwards I heard rough voices coming in my direction and I knew that my instincts had been proven right: I was being pursued. While I knew that I had nothing worth stealing, I also knew that robbers often turned violent if they found nothing of value on their victims. As the voices drew nearer I held my breath in fear, but then to my relief I heard the voices start to fade into the distance, but kept perfectly still and quiet in my den.

After some time had passed, I gave a sigh of relief that the danger had gone, but I was still very aware that the thugs may still be wandering around the docks. Taking stock of my situation, I decided that my den of old fish crates was at least protecting me from the rain and keeping me concealed, so I settled down as best I could for the night. Cold and wet as I was, sleep soon overtook me and the next thing I heard was the sound of the gulls circling the harbour in the cold grey light of dawn. As I emerged from my den of fish crates, the harbour appeared more or less deserted with only a few dockworkers hanging around, who hardly spared me a look as I shuffled by. I decided that this was no place to try and beg for my breakfast, so I followed the road until I found a more likely spot by a shop and sat down with my haiga of the whooper swans in front of me beside my begging bowl.

My efforts were soon rewarded when a rather poor looking woman came out of the shop and stopped to look at my haiga. Her face showing the signs of a long life of hardship as she peered at my work. Then she gave a gruff little sound, which I took as a sign of her appreciation.

'Did you do this?' she asked.

'Yes,' I replied hopefully.

'All by yourself?' she asked, looking me straight in the eye.

'All by myself,' I replied, unable to suppress a smile.

'It's good,' she declared, dropping two little rice cakes into my begging bowl. Then she gave another gruff little sound of appreciation and, with a final glance at my work, went on about her business.

The rice cakes tasted delicious and as I sat there having breakfast, more people stopped to look and drop coins into my bowl. To my delight, the people of Honshu appeared to love haiga as much as the people of Hokkaido.

I scooped out some of the coins and went into the shop and bought a bowl of tea to celebrate my good fortune. Not only did things bode well for my journey down through the main island toward Mount Fuji, but I appeared to have become a haiga poet with people paying to see my work.

And so, I began the second stage of my pilgrimage, which would take me all the way down the east coast of Honshu. My life from this point seemed to take a turn for the better. With every mile covered and with every coin dropped into my bowl, my confidence grew in my ability to reach my goal and see the holy mountain in all its majestic beauty. The weather also improved with the coming of spring and it was a joy rather than a burden to walk along the coast taking in the sights.

As spring turned to summer, however, I had to spend some of the money I had earned from my haiga to buy a large-brimmed straw hat to shelter me from the fierce heat of the sun. By this time I had also taken to using a strong stick to support my legs. I must confess that with my hat and stick I began to see myself as something of a wandering poet. If the summer days were a bit over-tiring, the summer nights were an absolute delight as I lay under the stars dreaming of Mount Fuji-san.

As summer turned to autumn and I drew nearer to the holy mountain, some nights I would hardly sleep at all, with my imagination making mental pictures of what Fuji-san might look like. Although I had seen many images of the mountain, I knew that the reality must be infinitely more striking, to see it up close in all its majestic beauty. I knew that I was drawing close to reaching my goal because when people stopped to look at my haiga, I would ask them how far it was to Fuji-san. 'Not far,' they would reply, and point further along the coast.

One evening, as I was making my way along and brushing autumn leaves with my feet, I looked up and there in the distance stood the holy mountain in all its majesty. The sight literally took my breath away and my Japanese heart burned with love. Mount Fujiyama was ablaze in the glory of a perfect autumn evening, with a light fall of snow on its highest peak and its base covered in the golden fire of the autumn leaves. Such moments are the essence of haiku, and I sat down just where I was to write my haiku to Fuji-san.

Fuji-san painted a thousand haiku in my mind and I did not know where to begin. Thousands of famous Japanese artists and poets have tried to capture the beauty of the holy mountain. I could only surrender my heart to it and let the beauty of Fuji-san capture me.

I sat there in awed silence for a very long time until the sun began to set, and only then did I take out one of my little scraps of rice paper and write my haiku to the holy mountain.

Among autumn leaves
Fuji-san soars to heaven
flames of burning gold.

Happy with my work, I settled down with my back to a tree and let my eyes drink in the majestic beauty of the holy mountain dissolving in the liquid gold of sunset. Although physically tired after the last leg of my journey, a feeling of elation swept through me. I had accomplished what I initially thought to be impossible, I had walked over a thousand miles, overcome the Sea of Japan, and achieved my goal. I felt like someone who had climbed a mountain, rather than someone who had simply walked toward one. And so, as my eyes began to droop with tiredness, I curled up at the base of the tree and fell into a deep contented sleep.

A cool breeze awakened me in the middle of the night to behold a sight which I will never forget, the holy mountain bathed in moonlight. If it is possible to actually fall in love with a mountain, then I fell in love that night. Fuji-san was like a serenely beautiful Japanese lady, bathed in the blue of moonlight against a backdrop of stars.

'For the soul of the poet to blossom, it must look upon Fuji-san.' With his words echoing in my mind, I realised that I owed an eternal debt of gratitude to that old haiku poet who inspired me to set out upon this mind expanding journey.

5

Sitting in the snow
an old monk and a beggar
share an empty bowl.

Ame

I found the words of the old poet to be true every day as I gazed at the holy mountain in all its different moods: in the sun and the rain, in the day and the night, glistening in moonlight or shrouded in mist, it was the first thing I looked at every morning and the last thing I saw at night before falling asleep. And yes, I did feel my soul begin to blossom and my haiku deepen. Whatever lay in my future, I knew that the holy mountain would live forever in my soul.

I was not alone in my love for Fuji-san, as flocks of people streamed to the holy mountain every day, like autumn leaves flowing in a stream of colour, their faces reflecting their love for this most sacred place. As I sat by the roadside with my haiku to Fuji-san, many people stopped to read it and smile and drop coins in my bowl. I suppose seeing a haiku poet sitting on the slopes of the holy mountain was quite fitting. I did not feel bad about showing my haiku of Fuji-san to earn enough to eat. In a way it felt that the holy mountain was rewarding me for my long pilgrimage and I saw the joy it gave to other fellow travellers.

Sitting by the roadside, with my journey over and with all the time in the world, I watched this stream of people flowing by. Some would be dressed in expensive clothes and talk loudly about the beauty of Fuji-san to impress their listeners, while others would be more quiet and reflective as they took in the beauty of scene. I found the monks to be the most interesting, for they would find a quiet spot and just sit there for hours in contemplation of the holy mountain.

For me the beauty of Fuji-san lay in its perfect symmetry, an almost perfect triangle with the sides gracefully curving inward as they reached up into the peak of the mountain. And for this perfection to be the result of a weakness in the earth that allowed the chaotic eruption of a volcano is the essence of haiku, beauty emerging from fragility. The mountain is held to be holy, because its beauty seems to be so perfect that it must be the work of heaven, even more so when its peak is lost in the mystery of low lying cloud. A perfect haiku in the midst of an imperfect world, pointing toward heaven.

The beauty of Fuji-san inspired me to create a haiga by drawing a haikai image of the holy mountain on the haiku which I had written when I first arrived. I kept the haikai as simple as possible in keeping with the Zen tradition, little more than a few lines to capture the curve of the holy mountain and the autumn leaves at its base. Once again the people seemed to love the haiga even more than the haiku on its own and many more would stop and smile and put coins in my bowl.

Then one evening, just before I was going to put my begging bowl away and find somewhere to sleep, a lady stopped to look at my haiga. She took a lot longer than anyone else and I could see that she was really absorbing how the words reflected the image. She was quite small and unremarkable in appearance, but on closer inspection I noticed that her dark blue kimono was of a very high quality, as were her tiny shoes. She was clearly a lady of some refinement and had a keen eye for art.

'Is this your own work?' she asked in a very cultured voice.

'It is,' I replied, unable to hide the pride I took in the haiga.

'How much is it?' she asked, to my complete astonishment.

I had never even considered the possibility of someone actually buying my work. As I struggled to try and put a price on it, it slowly dawned upon me that I did not actually want to sell it. This beautiful creation was my personal response to the culmination of my pilgrimage to the holy mountain. It seemed somehow wrong to sell it.

'So sorry,' I heard myself say. 'But it means too much to me to sell.'

I could see the disappointment in her eyes, but she quite graciously said that she understood. With a last look at the haiga, she gave me a little bow and walked away. In yet another moment of inspiration, I got up and caught up with her again.

'If you wish, I could create a copy for you,' I said.

The lady smiled at me and said that would be very nice. So we went back to my spot together and she stood very patiently and still beside me as I copied my haiga on to the best piece of rice paper I could find. It did not take very long, as the essence of this art form is in its simplicity.

'Beautiful,' the lady said, when it was finished. 'How much?'

Once again I was completely taken aback. I had absolutely no idea.

'Whatever you think it is worth,' I replied.

'Thousand yen?' the lady asked, taking out a crisp 1000 yen note from her purse. More than enough to keep me going on food for a week.

'Domo origato,' I replied, handing over the copy and receiving my very first commission payment for my art, hardly able to believe that I was now a real haiga artist.

As the months went by and winter began to set in, the stream of pilgrims to the holy mountain began to slow to a trickle and my begging bowl began to take longer to fill. Until now the local officials had seemed quite happy for me to ply my trade as a haiku beggar on the site, but now as they passed me by I began to sense from their attitude that my welcome was beginning to wear thin. But what to do now? Having achieved my goal, what next? Should I simply return to Hokkaido?

At the thought of leaving the holy mountain to return home, however, I began to become aware of a sense of something remaining unfulfilled. And then I realised that although my Fuji-san experience had been greater than I could have ever imagined, there still remained in the depth of my heart the unanswered question of my ikigai. Yes my haiku had developed beautifully, but I still had the sense that there had to be something more for me to realise my reason for living.

I fell asleep that night with these questions running through my mind. As I awoke the next morning with a covering of frost on my coat, I was delighted to hear the unmistakable cry of my friends the whooper swans and looking up, I watched them flying south for the winter. I suddenly realised that to simply turn around and go back to Hokkaido, not only would I be walking into the harsh northern winter, but that I would be missing a golden opportunity to see the rest of Honshu.

As I watched the white swans fly across Fuji-san and fade into the distance, I realised that my mind was made up and that I would follow them south. I spent the rest of the day gazing at the holy mountain, letting it sink into my soul. Then as evening drew on, I sat in formal zazen to say sayonara to Mt. Fujiyama as the setting sun gave way to the tranquil blue of moonlight.

And so I set out on the third part of my journey all the way down to the tip of Honshu, with the winter closing in behind me. I had by this time travelled down through the whole of Hokkaido and around 800 miles down the east coast of Honshu, with another 200 miles or so still to cover before reaching the southern tip of the island. But I felt well rested after my stay at the holy mountain and ready to move on. And so I followed the whooper swans on their southern migration. I had never dreamed when I sat on the porch of the boathouse and watched the swans fly south that one day I would be following their migration.

By the time I arrived at the southern tip of Honshu, winter had set in. I was fortunate, however, that the winters in the south are nothing like those in the north of Hokkaido, which can be extremely severe. By now I had also grown accustomed to sleeping rough and was quite adept at finding good places of shelter.

The income from my haiku also remained steady and so I always had enough to eat. I was also fortunate in finding some very tranquil and beautiful spots to practice my art. By now I had gathered quite a collection of haiku. Although I knew them all by heart, I would sometimes lay them out on the ground before me to look at how my style was developing.

One day when I was looking at the one with the swans, I became aware that I was being watched by an old Zen monk. Taki-san had always taught me to be courteous and respectful to monks, so I immediately stood up and bowed to the venerable old man who smiled and bowed in return and said, 'O-ha-yo gozaimasu.'

I wished him good morning in return, then he drew nearer and asked if he could look at my treasure. Treasure seemed a strange word indeed to use for a wandering beggar's scraps of rice paper. The old monk must had read my mind or saw in my face what I was thinking, for he went on to say that he saw the way I looked on my collection and so for me they were quite obviously a treasure.

'These are fine works of art,' he said. 'And treasure indeed in that it comes from the soul, where true treasure is to be found – not the material kind, which only burdens the soul and holds it captive within the bonds of material illusion.'

I could only smile and bow again, as I had never entered into such a lofty discussion with a monk and didn't know what to say.

'It is the essence of Zen, my young haiku poet, to free the soul from the burden of material things,' he continued. 'To recognise the true beauty that lies beyond the material world. Your swans flying into the mist are beautiful, but suggest an even greater beauty of the soul flying up into the mystery that lies beyond this world.'

I found this old monk fascinating company as we sat together in the snow looking at my work and talking about Zen. He informed me that haiku had actually been invented as a form of Zen meditation, to train young monks on how to focus the mind upon the beauty of the moment and the essence of reality.

'I see that your begging bowl is empty,' he said, suddenly picking it up to look at it more closely. 'To the unenlightened mind it is of little worth, but to the enlightened mind it is treasure indeed. It is the way of Zen to seek the treasure hidden in every little thing.'

To my surprise, the old monk then began to fill my bowl with handfuls of snow until it was overflowing. 'The essence of a bowl is to be empty of itself,' he explained. 'Being overfull obscures its true nature and beauty.'

He then turned the bowl upside down leaving it empty again. 'This is the way of Zen,' he said, returning the bowl to me. 'To empty oneself from all the things that obscure our true nature, to free the soul to find enlightenment.'

I sat there in silence for a moment, holding my empty begging bowl and reflecting on what the old monk had said. 'Am I then like a Zen monk?' I asked. 'For my bowl and my life are almost always empty as I sit here with nothing.'

The old monk looked kindly at me for a moment, then slowly shook his head. 'Sadly no,' he replied. 'For your bowl is always full, of all the things you wish you had, but can never have.'

'Then how can I ever find happiness?' I asked.

'By becoming like your empty bowl,' he replied. 'By freeing yourself from all the desires which keep you from finding true happiness. I can see that you follow a very hard path through the world and have almost nothing. But I also see someone who may be on the way toward enlightenment and I humbly offer you this advice to help you on your way.'

'And may I ask if you have found enlightenment by following the way of Zen?' I asked.

The old monk became very silent and I began to fear that I had somehow offended him.

'The way of Zen prepares the mind to be open to recognise those fleeting moments of enlightenment that may appear,' he said finally. 'And I have been fortunate in catching a rare and fleeting glimpse of enlightenment from time to time. But the ultimate awakening of the mind and soul to the eternal perfection, which transcends the world, still remains elusive.'

As he said this, I saw him smile. 'Your question reminds me of a story,' he said. 'One day an old monk asked a novice monk why he spent so much of his time sitting in zazen meditation.

'"To achieve enlightenment," the novice replied. The old monk then sat down beside him and picking up a rough stone, began to rub it against his robe.

'"Why are you rubbing that stone against your robe?" asked the novice.

'"To polish it until it becomes a mirror of perfection," replied the old monk.

'"But that is impossible," said the novice. "You could sit there forever and never turn a stone into a mirror."

'"True," replied the old monk. "But I thought I might join you so that we could both sit here and try to achieve the impossible together."'

The old monk and I laughed at his Zen story, then a natural silence fell between us for a long moment until the old monk got slowly back to his feet again.

'I wish you well on your path through life my young friend,' he said. 'And may you find enlightenment when you reach your journey's end. But as you travel, remember that the Zen monk does not fix his mind on the end, but learns to travel in peace in the here and now, to be at one with yourself and with the moment. Zen does not tell you what to do, only how to be. The practice of Zen will help you to walk in peace and harmony with all things, for that is your true Zen nature.'

We said sayonara, then we bowed and I watched him go. I knew that I would never forget our meeting or my first lesson from a Zen master.

That night I lay awake looking at the lights burning warmly in people's homes and thinking of all the love and warmth within them. I realised that the old monk's words were very true and that my bowl was indeed full of desires which a wandering beggar could never achieve. If I was ever to achieve happiness, then I must look inside myself to find it, and perhaps that is where I had also to look to find my ultimate ikigai. Before falling asleep I resolved to take his advice to embrace my empty bowl and my way of life, to search for that illusive happiness of enlightenment.

6

An ocean of stars
tenderly touching the soul
beauty beyond words.

Ame

The next morning after my meeting with the Zen monk, I awoke with a sense of peace and a lightness of spirit, resolved to embrace a life of simplicity. While my life had not changed in the material sense, internally I felt I had a new purpose, to emulate the old monk who had taught me that the way to find happiness and fulfillment was not to seek after material things but to be free of them. As a wandering beggar, I therefore had a golden opportunity to walk in the way of Zen and seek enlightenment.

On the horizon, the winter sunshine filled me with a feeling of fresh energy to pursue my new way of life. Choosing a good spot, I took out my very first haiku to mark my new beginning, the one about the beggar and the butterfly. Holding it out, I waited with my begging bowl before me. Within a few moments a young woman stopped to read it, then smiled at me and dropped enough money into my bowl to pay for my breakfast.

I took this as a sign of good fortune for my new adventure as I enjoyed my morning tea and rice cakes. With the sun shining above me and the sea before me I felt as free as the wind, with the whole of Japan just waiting for me to discover its beauty.

After breakfast I decided to change the haiku into a haiga. With a few simple lines, I drew a beggar and a butterfly on it, then sat back to take it in. It seemed to me to emulate my new adventure, with me as the beggar following the butterfly of enlightenment as it danced before me just out of my reach.

Once again the passers-by seemed to like it just as much as I did and I soon had more than enough to see me through the day. I was then free to simply walk along in the beauty of the moment, taking in the winter sunshine, the ice blue of the sea and the freshness of the morning air, just like a Zen monk in search of enlightenment.

I spent my winter there at the southern tip of Honshu, until one morning I awoke to the sound of the whooper swans on their migration north again from the island of Kushu where they had wintered. I watched them with delight, listening to their calls which appeared to be filled with a sense of joy, as though happy to be starting their migration back to Hokkaido. Watching the swans stirred something in my heart and I found myself remembering how I used to sit on the porch of the boathouse watching them fly in to land in our bay. In that moment, I realised that it was time for me also to return home.

With the first signs of spring, I began my own migration following the whooper swans north. The island of Honshu is over one thousand miles long, but I had already travelled that distance down the east coast and so I was confident that I would be able to complete the return journey by the west coast and then carry on north through Hokkaido until I eventually reached home.

I had been forced to leave the boathouse out of necessity to survive, but now I was returning with a new sense of confidence in my ability to find enough to live on each day from displaying my haiku and haiga. The thought of being in my own home again began to be very appealing. All the simple things which I loved came flooding back to my mind: sitting on the porch watching the whooper swans, watching the sun set over the sea, lying on my tatami at night listening to our old boat rocking against the oak jetty. And so, with these things in mind, I set out on my return journey home.

First, I had the small matter of a thousand miles through Honshu to cover before I could even get on the ferry for Hokkaido. If anything, the west coast of Honshu proved to be even more beautiful than the east coast. As I slowly made my way north, the landscape unfolded before me with scene after scene of breathtaking beauty. I discovered a myriad of idyllic little coves where I would sit watching turquoise blue waves rolling onto golden shores. At night, I would lay awake gazing up at an endless ocean of stars with a thousand haiku running through my mind about this beautiful land.

As the seasons changed from spring to summer, Japan continued to unfold the secrets of her beauty to me. The illusive butterfly of enlightenment, however, remained beyond my grasp. Occasionally I would catch a fleeting glimpse of something transcendent, for example in the way the sunlight would dance upon the crest of an incoming wave to create jewel like droplets of spray, or on perfectly still nights how the stars seemed to float upon the ocean. At such times, it was as though there was something just beneath the surface of this beauty that was even more elusively beautiful. In Japan we say that such things are ten kara no, heavenly. The more I saw of these things, the more I became convinced that the old Zen monk was absolutely right in his belief that in emptying oneself of material distractions the mind becomes open to see the true treasures that are all around us.

Somewhere along that mind expanding journey, I truly began to see my poor way of life as a hidden blessing, opening my mind to the transcendent beauty of life in all its simple perfection. I felt that my haiku had also matured with every new experience and began to deepen and touch upon more spiritual insights.

I noticed also that people would take longer to read my haiku before dropping something into my bowl, and even look into my eyes to let me see how my words had touched something within them. To me this was even more rewarding than money, a recognition of me as a haiku poet. And now I was returning to Hokkaido from this journey of self discovery with a treasure beyond riches, little scraps of rice paper with the soul of Japan written in Haiku.

7

Alone in the night
listening to falling rain
an ocean of tears.

Ame

As summer turned to autumn, I continued north. I still had a very long way to go and was becoming more aware of the toll that this epic journey had taken upon me. My legs, which have never been strong, were becoming increasingly weak and I was leaning more and more on my stick. With the changing of the seasons, I began to realise that winter may well overtake me before I reached the Hokkaido coast. But then something else happened that almost brought my journey to an end.

One evening while I was begging in a town, three louts began to laugh at me and call me wareta, broken. As usual I took no notice and just kept my head down, looking at a haiku I had just written. Then one of them came over, grabbed the haiku out of my hand and read it aloud; he then tore it up and threw it to the wind and they all began laughing and shouting 'wareta' at me again.

I was more afraid than angry, but there was nothing I could do other than sit there with my head down. This only seemed to encourage them and they began to slap me around the head and continue to hurl insults at me. I have never been able to fight, so I could only cover my head with my hands and curl up into a ball on the ground. They then began to beat me harder, punching and kicking me. I felt the blows go deep and I began to fear for my life.

Then I heard a man say, 'Leave him alone.' He did not shout, but there was something in his voice that stopped the louts immediately. I looked up from behind my hands to see a rather small middle-aged gentleman calmly facing the three louts. Although small, he stood very erect with his hands loosely at his side, his eyes locked unblinkingly on the louts, as though poised and ready for action.

The louts appeared uncertain how to react to this challenge, but then they started to laugh and shout insults at the man, threatening to beat him up also. The small man said nothing and just calmly stood his ground without taking his eyes off them for a second. There was an air of stillness and assurance about him as one who was shoaku suru, in complete control.

The louts continued to shout insults at him but I noticed that they did not dare try to come near him. Then some other passers-by came over to see what was happening and at this the three louts decided to leave, shouting insults and threats at the small man, who just calmly watched them go. He then knelt down and helped me up to a sitting position.

'Have they hurt you?' he asked.

'I'm all right,' I lied, for I was on the point of collapse.

Someone offered me some water, which I took while the small man ran his hands over me.

'No bones broken,' he said with a smile. 'But you are far from all right. I think we need to get you home.'

I thanked him for helping me and then explained my situation to him, that I was begging my way north to return home. To my complete surprise, this total stranger said that in that case I should let him take me back to his house to rest.

'My name is Oshiro,' he said, helping me to my feet and giving me my stick. 'My house is not far. Can you manage to walk?'

I assured him that I could, but I was still glad of his support on my other arm as I hobbled along with my stick. When we got to his house, Oshiro introduced me to his wife Fujiko, who immediately sat me down and began to tend to my cuts and bruises, while Oshiro set about making some tea. I was completely overwhelmed by their kindness, especially after just experiencing how cruel people could be.

As Fujiko finished tending my wounds and Oshiro laid out the tea, I took the opportunity to thank him once again for his bravery in being prepared to fight off my three attackers.

'Oshiro-san fight?' Fujiko laughed. 'He has never fought in his life.'

I was very surprised to hear this and confessed that I thought that he must be some form of martial arts master, the way he faced the three louts.

'Good heavens no, Ame-san,' Oshiro said. ' I am a tea master. I do hope the tea is to your liking,' he said, handing me a bowl of tea.

At this we all began to laugh, which I had to quickly stop because of the pain in my ribs.

'A hot bath will help,' Fujiko said. 'Please finish your tea while I prepare it for you.'

The tea was delicious and began to revive me a little and by the time Fujiko returned, I was feeling a bit less shaken by the attack. However, she still insisted on helping me to my feet, then gently taking my arm led me around to their little bath house.

The hot bath was heavenly, even though I must confess that I was more than a little embarrassed when this very beautiful Japanese lady helped me out of my dirty old clothes and into the water.

Fujiko then left me to soak in the deliciously hot bath. I had not had a bath since leaving the boathouse, and even then it had only ever been the old tub, which Taki-san would take the chill off with a few pots of hot water. In contrast as I lay in this luxury, I felt as though I had gone to heaven. After walking all around the coast of Japan, it felt like my tired body was floating on a cushion of air.

Fujiko returned and help me out of the bath, and to my embarrassment once again helped to dry me and then dress me in a soft kimono.

'Now Ame-san, a massage,' she said, and in a way that offered no option to refuse. 'And there is no need to feel shy because I am a trained shiatsu isha and you need this to help your wounds to heal.'

With no way to refuse, I lay down on the tatami and surrendered to the shiatsu. Fujiko's hands seemed to be able to feel every part of my body that ached and would linger there until the pain eased before moving sensitively on to the next area of pain. As the pain seemed to dissolve away, I began to feel a sense of relaxation and peace running through my body, like a stream of healing water washing away all the stress and fatigue that had accumulated since I left the boathouse. But there was something else, something even deeper in the touch of those gentle hands.

While I had experienced many acts of kindness from strangers, as this lovely lady with the scent of jasmine in her sleek black hair continued to massage my pain away, I became acutely aware that I had not been touched by another human being since the day that Taki-san had touched my face shortly before she died.

As I realised this, I felt my heart melt and tears began to flow down my face. By some form of feminine wisdom, Fujiko seemed to understand this and very gently touched my face and held her hand there in perfect silence for a very long time. There was no need for words; she instinctively seemed to know that what I needed was someone to simply touch me.

Later that evening we sat down to a beautifully prepared traditional Japanese meal by lamplight. My hosts showed great interest in my journey all around the coast of Japan and in particular in the haiku I had created on my way.

Fujiko said that she loved the one about the beggar and the butterfly, and so I went on to describe my meeting with the beautiful geisha that had inspired it. Fujiko then asked me to copy it out again for her to keep in memory of me. When I handed it to her she took it in both her hands and touched it to her forehead in the most formal way, then gave me such a beautiful look that I will never forget.

I felt that it was my turn then to bow formally and thank Oshiro and Fujiko for their great kindness, and in particular for Oshiro's bravery in saving me from the attack. I said that it was even more brave of him to have faced down my three attackers without any martial arts training. Oshiro made little of this, saying that he was never in any real danger as cowards like that always backed down when confronted by anyone who appeared ready for them.

'You must hear the tale of the cha-no-u master and the samurai,' Oshiro said, and began to tell me the story.

One day, a cha-no-u master met a samurai on a narrow bridge and because the old tea master did not stand aside quickly enough, the samurai challenged him to a duel.

'Be back here tomorrow at dawn with a sword or I will seek you out and kill you,' said the samurai.

The old tea master had never held a sword in his life, but went to the house of a friend of his who was also a samurai to ask him for a loan of a sword to try and defend himself.

'If you go near this samurai with a sword he will surely kill you,' advised his old friend. 'Let us have tea together and try to think of what we must do.'

As the samurai watched his old friend take his tea, he saw the fear leave him and the tea master's serenity return.

'You have no need of a sword to meet this samurai,' declared his old friend. 'You are a master of cha-no-u and can meet this rogue with nothing but your serenity of spirit and strength of character.'

The next morning, the old tea master set out to follow his friend's advice. As he stood before his aggressor once again on the bridge, he imagined the samurai to be a guest at the tea ceremony. He thought of nothing except the gentle breeze on his face and the sound of the water trickling under the bridge as he waited for the samurai to attack.

The samurai was astonished to see this profound old man standing before him with nothing but a serene smile on his face. Recognizing that he was in the presence of a master, the samurai immediately bowed down and begged forgiveness for his behaviour.

'So you see, Ame-san,' Oshiro concluded, 'when faced with aggression it was his strength of character, rather than physical strength which defeated his attacker. And as a master of cha-no-u, I was not completely helpless when I faced those three cowards who attacked you.'

'That's all very well, Oshiro-san,' Fujiko said. 'But we must not tire out our guest with any more of your cha-no-u stories. And Ame-san, we insist that you spend the night here with us as our guest.'

I was so touched by their kindness that I could only bow again in thanks, and then wishing Oshiro goodnight, followed Fujiko who showed me along to my room.

'I do hope you will be comfortable here, Ame-san,' she said as she arranged my tatami. And then she became very quiet, as though trying to decide something. 'Ame-san,' she said finally looking at me very tenderly. 'I feel that I must tell you something. During our shiatsu session, I did all that I could to restore the balance of your ki energy to help you recover.'

'Thank you, Fujiko-san,' I replied. 'I have never experienced anything as wonderful as that in all my life.'

'I am so glad,' she said. 'But I feel that I must tell you, Ame-san, that your ki energy, your life force is so very weak. I fear that if you continue to lead this very hard way of life on the road, then you may not have very long in this world. So sorry, Ame-san.'

It's not easy to hear that your life may be ending when you have hardly begun to live. It was the last thing I had expected to hear after such a pleasant evening. But while I had never regretted my decision to set out on this epic journey, as the time went by I was becoming more aware of the toll that this rough living was taking upon my health. All I could do was thank Fujiko for her honesty and to reassure her that I now planned to return home to the boathouse and try to settle down there.

'Please do, Ame-san,' she said. Then she touched my face once again and wished me o-yasumi nasai. I wished her goodnight in return and watched her leave, stopping to bow very formally to me before sliding the door screen closed.

As I lay there in the comfort of a fresh tatami with a roof over my head and perfect safety, I realised that it was indeed time for me to go home and that I would most probably not survive another winter on the road. With luck, I could earn enough from my haiku to survive. If not, then at least I would end my life where I had known such happiness with Taki-san.

With my mind on returning home and settling down, my thoughts turned once again to the question of finding my ikigai. Did my life have to have some special meaning? Or was life simply about getting by each day and making the most of what little comforts came your way? With these doubts running through my mind, I surrendered to the comfort of my warm tatami and fell asleep.

I awoke the next morning to find that my dirty clothes had all been washed and pressed and folded neatly by my tatami. Despite my thoughts before falling asleep, I now felt refreshed and confident once again to continue on my way. After a very good breakfast, I thanked Oshiro and Fujiko once again for their wonderful kindness to me and prepared to take my leave.

'It was our honour to have a haiku poet as our guest,' Fujiko said. 'And we insist that before you go, you join us in the tea ceremony.'

The couple then led me along a small winding path through their traditional garden to their cha-no-u house. I noticed that the stoned path had been freshly sprinkled with water and Oshiro explained that this was to symbolise how one should honour the guest invited to the tea ceremony by making everything clean and fresh.

Before entering the cha-no-u house we washed our hands and face from a small bamboo bowl. Oshiro explained that this was to symbolise how we should cleanse our minds from all distractions of the outside world and focus simply on the here and now of this moment.

Stooping low to enter the small door, to remind those who enter of the need for humility, Oshiro invited Fujiko and I to sit on the simple tatami. He then explained that the cha-no-u ceremony focused on the key principles of life, which were harmony, respect, purity and tranquility. He then began the simple ceremony of making tea for his guests. Simple but incredibly profound, with every gesture a perfection achieved from a lifetime of practice, truly a master at work in which we left the outside world behind us as we delighted in the moment.

After the ceremony, Oshiro thanked me for being his guest and explained that another key principle of cha-no-u was that each ceremony was a totally unique moment that could never be repeated, the principle of ichigo ichie, literally meaning one time one moment.

'We have now shared such a unique moment, Ame-san,' he said. 'And Fujiko-san and I will never forget you.'

We bowed formally to each other as we said sayonara by the door of their house. As I took the coast road, I turned and saw them still standing at the door to watch me go. I gave this beautiful couple a final wave then followed the road north.

As I was leaving the outskirts of the town, all my feelings of happiness and serenity were suddenly broken, like a knife cutting into my soul, as up ahead of me I saw one of the thugs who had attacked me lounging against the wall. It was the smallest and nastiest of the group, his face breaking into an ugly sneer as he recognised me and slowly and deliberately started toward me.

In one swift stroke, all the self-esteem which Oshiro and Fujiko had fostered within me by their kindness and respect was taken away and replaced by the cold fear of being ridiculed and beaten once again. I felt myself begin to cower away from the imminent attack, feeling my legs give way to let me curl upon the ground. But then something stirred deep within me, something deeper than my fear, a cold anger at this thug who was set upon making me cower in submission before him.

With a strength of resolve that I never knew I possessed, I made my legs stand firm and standing my ground, I faced this thug with my eyes locked upon him, just as my friend Oshiro had done. As the thug closed in on me, I suddenly saw a look of hesitation creep into his eyes. I must have looked a terrible sight, with my face all bruised and my eyes staring with cold hatred into his.

To my complete astonishment, the thug stopped his advance. While he started to shout insults at me, he still kept his distance as I faced him in silent contempt. Then, with a final flourish of sneers and insults, he laughed at me and walked away.

As the blood slowly returned to my face, I took a deep breath of exhilaration at my victory over this coward; Oshiro's story of the tea master's victory over the samurai came to my mind, for I too had overcome this bully with nothing but strength of character.

Nevertheless I still had the good sense to make my way as fast as I could away from the village, just in case the bully decided to return with his friends for revenge, because I had exposed his cowardliness even toward a crippled beggar.

I made myself a promise that day. Never again would I cower on the ground from an attack; come what may, I would stand my ground. I had discovered an inner strength of character that I did not know I possessed, revealed by the simple kindness and respect of two people whom I shall never forget.

I quickly discovered, however, that even after all that Fujiko's massage had done for me, the beating that I had taken had left me very weak indeed. After only a mile or two, I had to stop and rest for an hour before going on again, with each step taking its toll upon me.

It was dark before I had covered less than five miles and still no sign of the next town or village on the horizon. I realised that I could go no further and, finding some shelter in some thick bushes, curled up for the night.

As I lay there in the cold, I remembered the comfort of Oshiro and Fujiko's house and then to make things even worse it began to rain. I felt utterly miserable and so terribly alone, after the gentle and gracious company I had so recently received. But then in that most utterly miserable situation, Japan chose to reveal yet another aspect of her serene beauty to me. The dark clouds that had filled the sky suddenly parted to reveal a most perfect full moon, which turned the rain into silver as it fell into the sea. In that moment of breathtaking beauty, I forgot all about my miseries and lay there with my mind capturing this fleeting moment for eternity in haiku.

Softly by moonlight
raindrops falling to the sea
the tears of heaven.

8

As the beggar sleeps
in the silence of the night
the first fall of snow.

Ame

As the days went by and the pain from my attack eased, I began once again to appreciate the beauty which my vagabond way of life had opened up to me. Japan continued to unfold before me like an ancient scroll of haiku. I transformed the tears of heaven haiku into a haiga by letting raindrops fall onto the paper to create a misty effect, to highlight the rain dissolving into the sea. People seemed to love it as much as I did and were generous whenever I displayed it. I sometimes like to think that it was a little gift from heaven to me that night when I was feeling so lonely and miserable.

It was almost winter when I finally made my way back to the north of Honshu and the ferry port where I had begun my journey around the island. After yet another cold night sleeping in the shelter of the same old fish crates, I made my way back on to the ferry for Hokkaido.

As I stood at the front of the boat watching Hokkaido take shape from the sea, my heart was full of feelings about coming home and longing once again to sit on the porch of the boathouse. I suppose sometimes you have to leave a place before you can really appreciate how beautiful it really is.

I was not home yet, however, because I estimated that I still had some two hundred miles or so to cover along the west coast to reach my village. I now began to wonder how I might be treated by the villagers on my return. After all, it was because of their turning away from me that I had been compelled to leave in the first place and beg my way around the other towns and villages.

Would displaying my haiku make any difference? Would they continue to avoid me and walk by without even stopping to look? I was set in my own mind that come what may, I would live out my life in the boathouse. I would write my haiku in my own home and spend my days drawing haikai of the swans in our bay.

As I made my way north, the weather began to take a turn for the worse, with darkening skies and frosty mornings. Then one grey evening, to my delight I heard the sound of whooper swans and watched as their white wings took shape from the dark grey clouds. They had started their southern migration to escape the approaching Hokkaido winter. I watched them go until their plaintiff call drifted away on the wind. Then I turned my face north again and continued on my way.

The weather deteriorated with every passing day, the temperature dropping continually. The nights were the hardest; I huddled against the wind in any scrap of shelter I could find, imagining what it would be like to sit by our old stove again to burn the driftwood that Taki-san and I had stored up.

The first snow began to fall while I was still over one hundred miles from home, and I could feel the intense cold taking its toll on my health. With no choice, I continued my slow advance from village to village.

One day, as I was begging by the harbour wall of a fishing village with my Tears of Heaven haiku on display, I had passed the time by watching an old fisherman sitting in his boat mending his nets. He struck me as being very much at peace as he worked away slowly with his eyes gazing out to sea.

He reminded me of the times when Taki-san and I used to do the same in our old boat after a day's fishing. The thought crossed my mind if only I had not been born so weak, perhaps I too could have carried on our family tradition and lived happily as a simple fisherman.

I continued to watch the old fisherman at his tasks until he finally stowed his nets in the stern of the boat. As he made his way past me, he stopped and looked down at my haiku.

'Did you do this?' he asked, after looking at it for some time.

'I did,' I replied. 'After watching the rain in the moonlight falling into the sea.'

'This is good, you know,' he said, looking at it again. 'Very good. You should show it to the haiku master.'

'The haiku master?'

'He lives just up there,' the old man said, pointing up the hill. 'Last little house on the right. I'm sure he would be interested in seeing it.'

With nothing to lose, I thanked the old fisherman and, following his directions, I came to a small traditional house at the top of the hill looking out to sea, which struck me as a perfect place for a haiku master.

Summoning up all my courage, I knocked on the door and waited until eventually I heard slow footsteps from inside and a venerable old man with a wispy white beard opened the door. I recognised him instantly as the old haiku poet I had met that day on the beach and who had inspired me to set out on my journey to see Fuji-san. I bowed formally and wished him Ohayo-gozimasu. He returned my greeting then peered at me intently for a moment.

'Do I know you?' he asked.

'We met on the beach a long time ago, haiku master,' I said. 'And you gave me advice on my haiku.'

'The young haiku poet!' he exclaimed with a smile. 'Pebbles on the beach, wasn't it?'

'It was,' I replied, delighted that he remembered me. 'And do you remember saying that for the soul of the haiku poet to blossom, it must look upon Fuji-san?'

'Yes, I believe I do,' he said. 'And have you done so?'

'I have just returned, haiku master,' I replied, unable to hide my pride.

'But then you must come out of the cold and have some tea,' he said. 'And tell me all about it, do please come in.'

This was indeed an unexpected pleasure and the thought of taking tea with a real haiku master was a real delight. His house was immaculately clean and very simply furnished in the traditional style. The cedar floor was highly polished and even though I had taken off my shoes, I still felt ashamed as my dirty old socks left marks upon it. The old haiku poet didn't appear to mind, or at least he was too polite to show it.

'Please be seated, my young friend,' he said, showing me to a small highly polished wooden satsuru. 'Forgive me, but I don't even know your name, do I?'

When I introduced myself, he told me that his name was Shijin, which simply means poet.

'A fine name for a haiku master,' I said.

'I have no other,' he said. 'I was found by monks, close to death. They nursed me back to life, but the memory of who I was or where I came from has never returned. And so I am simply Shijin, a poet.'

Shijin prepared tea and rice cakes for us, then showed great interest in my adventures and my accounts of the haiku I had created on the way.

'And now you have made your way all around Japan and returned to Hokkaido as a haiku poet,' he said. 'And now I must see something of your work, Ame-san.'

'This is the one which the old fisherman suggested that you would be interested in,' I said, rather self-consciously showing him the Tears of Heaven, which Shijin took from me very respectfully with both hands before intently pondering over it for a long moment.

'Very simple,' he said, finally looking up from the haiku.

I must confess that I felt very disappointed that the haiku master had found my work simple, and I must have let it show on my face.

'Very simple, Ame-san,' he said again. 'And very beautiful. The way haiku should be. You have captured the moment and the mystery perfectly. It is an honour to have read it. I can see that the soul of the poet has indeed looked upon Fuji-san. May I see some more of your work?'

Fishing around in my pockets, I eagerly laid out my collection of haiku, which now looked very tattered and rainsoaked against his highly polished tebaru. But the old poet picked each one up with great respect as though they were priceless treasures. For what seemed a very long time, he pondered over them, with me trying to read his expressions after each one. Finally, when he had read the last, he joined his hands together under his chin as he gazed steadily at me.

'These are exceptionally fine haiku, young man,' he said. 'You do indeed have talent. And there is a fragrance about them which I find quite unique.'

'A fragrance, haiku master?' I asked, trying to contain my happiness.

'A haiku term. It refers to an underlying theme running through a poet's work which can be quite distinctive. For example, one could recognise a haiku from one of the great masters even if it was not signed, simply by the fragrance. In your case, young man, although it is subtle and reflects your youth, there is a fragrance of shall we say mystery about your haiku. Which is quite charming.'

'Domo-origato, Shijin-san,' I replied, bowing formally as I did not know quite how to respond. I was of course delighted that a real haiku master had found my work impressive. In my enthusiasm, I confessed to him that my goal was now to live a life of simplicity in the boathouse and perhaps even one day to become a haiku master also.

'I would be most grateful, haiku master,' I continued, 'if you could enlighten me on how I too may become a master?'

But at this, Shijin slowly shook his head. 'So sorry, Ame-san, but it is impossible,' he said. 'You already know all I could teach you. Only haiku can teach you now how to become a master. But when you see your soul in your haiku, on that day you will have become a master of haiku.'

Before I said sayonara to Shijin, he showed me around his small traditional garden, with a little cherry tree beside a small stream which flowed under a little ornate wooden bridge. As we stood on the bridge watching leaves drift along the stream, Shijin appeared deep in thought for a moment.

'Haiku reveals eternity as a moment and a moment as an eternity,' he said finally. 'For what are we but leaves flowing in a stream of time? In haiku we can only try to capture fleeting glimpses of this most transient beauty. But most often such moments are beyond words, Ame-san.'

'Then how can we capture them?' I asked.

'By keeping our words as simple as possible,' he replied. 'Like a clear running stream, to try and reveal the beauty which lies beneath the surface of the water.'

Before allowing me to leave, Shijin said that he wanted to give me something by which to remember our second meeting. Once again I had the honour to watch a real haiku master at work. Sitting down by his tebaru, he paused to collect his thoughts for a moment. Then he let his brush fly across the rice paper and I watched in fascination as the haiku took shape with such apparent ease. He then signed it and handed it to me.

Watching drifting leaves,
haiku poets by a stream,
quiet reflections.
Shijin

'You do not know where your young life will lead,' he said. 'And I do not know where I have come from. Two leaves, flowing in a stream of time. Please keep this in memory of our time here.'

We said sayonara at his door and then he watched me go as I made my way back down the hill again. As I turned to look back, Shijin waved goodbye then bowed very formally and went back into his little house. It struck me that he too, like the old fisherman that I had observed in his boat, seemed very much at one with his simple way of life. No doubt the secret of their happiness lay in their finding their ikigai, their reason for living. With these thoughts in my mind, I turned north once again to try and find my own.

My meeting with Shijin had given me confidence in my ability to earn my living as a haiku poet back at the boathouse. The old poet had been so positive about my work that I now began to seriously consider if this could indeed be my ikigai.

Perhaps Taki-san had been right all along in her persistence that I should write haiku. How strange, though, that it took a chance meeting with an old poet to inspire me to set out on a journey of self discovery. And how strange that I should meet him once again by chance on my return journey home to reflect upon the skill I had developed on the way.

9

Alone in the woods
in the stillness of the night
a light in the dark.
Ame

As I continued north, the Hokkaido winter began to gather around me with every passing mile, like some malignant elemental force trying to prevent me reaching home. As I leaned into the icy driving wind, I set my mind on the boathouse, where I too like Shijin could sit in my own house and write haiku in peace and tranquility and no longer be like the fallen leaf in his haiku, drifting at the mercy of the elements.

I continued to make slow progress until the worst of the Hokkaido winter hit the north west coast in a terrible blizzard, with the driving snow making any progress impossible. I was left with no choice but to abandon the coast road and make my way inland to take shelter in the trees.

This was something that I had always tried to avoid by keeping to the coast roads, as danger lay up there in the woods where wolves roamed free. As I cautiously made my way further up into the trees, I finally found refuge in the hollow of a long dead oak tree, where I lay shivering with cold until sheer exhaustion overtook me and I fell asleep.

I do not know how long I slept there but when I awoke with the cold, night had fallen and I was covered in a thick blanket of snow. Shaking myself out of the hollow of the oak tree, I looked around to try and get my bearings. The snow had stopped and the wind had died down, but I had no idea how to get back the way I had come. I found myself hopelessly disorientated with no idea how to return to the coast.

I began to fear that I was going around in circles, the deep snow sapping any reserves of strength I had left in my legs. Just as I was nearing the limit of my endurance, the malignant howl of the wolf forced me on until I found this old hut in which I have now taken refuge for the night. If I had not found this shelter, then I seriously doubt if I would have survived the night and I would never reach my goal of returning home to the boathouse.

I remain physically exhausted on the floor of this old hut, but my mind feels somehow rested and at peace, for there is a tranquility about this old place that somehow gets beneath the skin. Being lost and alone in the woods in the dead of the night, I should feel a little anxious, but I feel strangely content, even happy to spend the night here. Sleep, however, escapes me; I am content to rest my eyes on the light from my akari, as it radiates a least a sense of warmth within the hut.

By the light of my akari, I go through my haiku collection and stop at the one that Shijin gave me about our lives being like leaves flowing in a stream of time. While I have very few possessions – a bowl, an akari, my collection of haiku – I realise that I remain very attached to them and would find it very difficult to let them go. I smile as I remember that I also actually own a boathouse, which I have grown to love even more for being parted from it for so long. So, I still have a long way to go to achieve the Zen ideal of detachment from material things that the old Zen monk spoke about.

My eyes fall on the little broken pot which I rescued from out of the snow, and I realise that I seem to have acquired yet another little treasure, because there is something about the little pot that touches my heart, for we are both wareta, broken. As I pick up the old pot and hold it in my hands, every crack and break seems to tell the story of its rough treatment before finally being thrown out as useless. Perhaps being wareta myself makes me more sensitive to such things, or perhaps this is the way all poets see things.

As a poet, I have developed a sense of the healing power of words, but sometimes silence can be even more powerful than words and touch the heart in ways that words never can. And now in some strange way I feel that this little broken pot in my hands seems to be telling me in its own silent way that we are all broken one way or another.

For the first time in my life, I actually see now that if I had not been broken, then I would not have taken to the road as a wandering beggar and would not have become a haiku poet. Perhaps my reason for being alive, my ikigai, is actually in some mysterious way bound together with my brokenness, for this is part of who I am and what has made me the person I have become. Someone who understands that in being broken, we feel more deeply the need to give and to receive care and compassion.

With this quite stunning realization, I just sit here in the middle of nowhere gazing at this little broken pot with new eyes, as it rests in my hands like a little bird with a broken wing. While it is clearly too badly broken to be of any further use as a pot, there remains a fragile beauty about it, even though the light from my akari seems to highlight all its imperfections. Then it suddenly occurs to me that my akari might actually fit quite nicely inside the pot.

As I put my akari into the broken pot, I find that it fits perfectly. And now the light streams out from every crack and crevice, transforming this useless little broken thing into a little kintsukuroi. I feel this thing of such fragile beauty touching my soul, because with the light inside, it no longer looks broken and its fragility only highlights its sense of translucent beauty, like a symbol of inner healing. As I hold this little silent haiku in my hands, I almost feel that we were destined to meet, like soulmates, completing one another.

In Japan, we traditionally make kintsukuroi out of broken pots by mending the cracks with molten gold. These are held in great esteem as valuable works of art, far superior than they ever were before they became broken. Rather than try to hide the way the cracks have been mended, they are celebrated in gold to show the pots unique character. It now strikes me that my little broken pot has undergone a similar transformation, but with light rather than gold being poured through the cracks.

As a haiku poet, I have often noticed how the most beautiful haiku are often touched with a shadow of sadness, which elevates them from the others by giving them a sense of depth and poignant beauty, reminiscent of the transient beauty of our fragile lives. The wonderful thing about the greatest haiku is their ability to speak to the soul in a way that actually transcends the words, like one soul speaking silently to another.

Sitting here with this little living haiku glowing warmly in my hands, it seems to speak to my soul once again, in its own silent way. It tells me that I do not have to be afraid or ashamed of being broken, because it is through my brokenness that I will perhaps help others to become whole through reading my haiku.

As I sit here in the middle of nowhere, in the stillness of the night with nothing but this little broken pot to keep my company, I realise that at this moment in time there is nowhere else that I would rather be. A feeling of peace washes over me and I close my eyes and surrender to sleep.

I do not know how long I have slept like that, with the broken pot in my hands, but it must have been quite some time, for the light has died out in my akari and the little pot has grown cold again. The old hut is now bathed in soft moonlight coming through the window. I feel very rested and at peace; there is a serenity here that I have not experienced in all my travels throughout Japan, even at Mount Fuji-san itself, which is revered in Japan as being a holy place.

In Japan we believe that certain places are shinsei-na, holy places where the veil that separates earth from heaven grows thin. While I have done nothing to deserve this, I now feel what I can only describe as a sense of holiness and that this old hut is actually such a place of shinsei-na.

I feel that I should perhaps say a prayer, but then the little broken pot speaks to me once again, in its own silent way, and I realise that there is no need to say or do anything, for I am loved, just as I am in all my brokenness. As I hold the broken pot in my hands, I feel that I too am being held in a feeling of love and compassion that transcends description.

I remember being held in love by my mother Taki-san and her whispering into my ear that God has hidden a secret in my heart that only I can discover. The secret I have found in this holy place, hidden in a little broken pot, is that there is an eternal beauty hidden within every human soul, which can sometimes only be seen when we are at our most vulnerable and fragile. It is then that the light within us shines out through all our brokenness to make us whole.

My mind goes back to the words of the old haiku poet and the old Zen monk, both of whom spoke of certain transient experiences that are beyond words. With nothing else to describe this feeling in the depth of my soul, I believe that here and now in this old hut I am experiencing what they spoke about. As my journey through Japan draws to its close, in this holy place I actually believe that I am now experiencing the greatest of all treasures, the spirit of enlightenment, which is amari-ni-utsukushii, too beautiful, even for haiku.

Even the moon shining through the window seems to be filled with a transcendent light that draws me out of the hut to look up into a perfectly clear night sky, ablaze with starlight that glistens upon a blanket of snow which covers everything in perfect stillness. Even the kabanoki trees appear to glisten in the starlight and the very air in my lungs seems to tingle with the freshness of snow.

I have always loved snow. For me it has always held a fascination. I remember as a child sitting on the porch of the boathouse in the evening with Taki-san at my side, watching huge soft snowflakes gently drifting down around us, like stars falling from heaven. I remember Taki-san's soft laughter at my fascination.

'It is only snow, Ame-san,' she had said. But for me it was something much more, for it brought with it a silence and a tranquility that was almost holy, like the fragile beauty of a sacrament.

As I stand here gazing up into an eternity of stars, I suddenly realise that with this perfectly clear moonlight I can now most probably find my way back to the coast. Something wonderful has happened to me in this holy place, something that will always be with me, but now I have this almost irresistible desire to see the boathouse once again and to sit on the porch in the snow and be near to Taki-san's place of rest by the two rocks.

By the light of the moon, I make my way up through the trees to a small rise in the landscape. There, to my delight, through a clearing in the trees I see the moonlight shining upon the Sea of Japan. But what makes my soul melt within me is the sight of the boathouse, covered in a blanket of snow. I can see the two rocks shimmering in the moonlight where Taki-san awaits my return. My journey has finally come to an end.

Suddenly I realise that in all this wonderful experience, I have actually left my akari and the broken pot back at the old hut. They both mean too much to me to leave behind and I must go back for them. But then as I turn around to make my way back, I realise that something is very wrong.

As I look for my footprints in the snow to retrace my steps, I see that the snow is untouched. There are no footprints. As my mind struggles to understand this, my heart begins to break as it slowly dawns upon me that I must be dreaming.

Then as I wait for this beautiful dream to end and the sight of the boathouse to disappear, across the moonlit sky a single whooper swan wings its way south. I watch in fascination, listening to its plaintiff call; this is no dream, for I have never felt more alive than I do at this moment.

The old haiku master said that when I see my soul in my haiku, then I too will have become a haiku master. I watch the swan spread its majestic white wings in the moonlight, like a soul making its way to the stars. Then I let my soul sing its haiku to heaven and fly up to follow the swan.

In a starlight sky
a swan sails across the moon
the wings of a soul.
Ame

BOOK TWO
1

Softly in the night
the whispering of the wind
the sound of the sea.

Taki

The moon casts its quiet light through the window of the boathouse as I awake to the sound of the tide lapping against the boat moored to the jetty just outside my room. I instinctively know that it will not be dawn for hours yet, but sleep evades me as I lay on my tatami looking at the blue and silver moon shadows playing on the old oak beams of the boathouse.

I truly love this old place; I was born here and will die here like the rest of my family for generations. The house is like a living family tree with all of its repairs to the oak beams and wooden roof at the hands of all the people who have lived here over the years. To me, all its little imperfect repairs make it even more beautiful, giving it a unique character, almost a personality all of its own.

Between the sounds of the tide lapping against our ancient fishing boat, I can hear Ame's gentle rhythmic breathing through the thin paper and wood screen which divides our sleeping areas. The pattern of his breathing tells me that he is still in a deep sleep and will probably sleep on until dawn.

The sound of the tide proves too much for me to resist and I carefully get up from my tatami, trying not to wake Ame. I gaze out of the window at the moonlight shining on the Sea of Japan, like a living Hokusai masterpiece. How I love this place. While Hokkaido is known for its severe winters and rugged landscapes, it is also breathtaking in it natural beauty.

The boat is rocking gently in the tide, as though trying to pull free from the old rope that holds it captive to one of the great oak timbers upon which the boathouse stands. I know that feeling; an almost irresistible desire to pull out into deep water. With a sigh, I surrender to the temptation and get dressed. I know that Ame will worry, as he does not like me taking the boat out on my own anymore, but the tide is pulling at my heart and I cannot resist.

Tiptoeing across the wooden floor, I hold my breath every time the old timbers creak and wait to hear if there is any change in Ame's breathing. I put a light to our little red akari and sit down at my tebaru to write him a short note, telling him not to worry, that I feel fine today and that I promise not to overexert myself. From the drawer of the tebaru I take out the last haiku I wrote about the moonlight on the water and pin it to the note. Ame loves my haiku and I hope this will give him something else to think about rather than worrying about me.

By the light of the akari I wrap up in my big heavy coat and scarf, then tip toe around the screen to look at Ame, curled up in a tight ball on his tatami. He has slept like this since he was a baby, even when I had to take him out in the boat with me, with him all wrapped up from the cold in the stern of the boat. I leave him to his dreams and head for the door.

No matter how carefully I tread, the ancient oak timber at the door creaks in protest, as it has done for years. My grandfather Yohji called it a cricket floor, which was a traditional thing in ancient Japan, built into the floor for the sound to warn against trespassers. But we have nothing for any trespasser to steal. We survive on what we catch in our boat. Our treasure lies in the simplicity of our lifestyle and in the absolute beauty of living in this old boathouse on the shore of this stunningly beautiful bay on the west coast of Hokkaido.

The night air is cold and crisp; it is still quite early spring and the cold of winter has not yet released its grip, but there was a red sunset over the bay last night, which usually promises a fine clear day. I wrap my coat tightly around me then step carefully down into the boat and take my seat, like sitting down with an old dear friend.

I untie the rope, then use the oar to push off from the jetty and let the boat glide silently away. As I look at my window, I see the dim red glow of the akari I left burning beside the note I left for Ame to be sure he finds it. Then I dip both oars in and pull away until I feel the breeze is strong enough and open up the sail, which billows out to get me underway.

Turning the boat along the coast, I pass the village to see a few little lights already glowing in some of the windows where the fishermen are getting an early start. Then the boat slips further along the coast, leaving the village in its wake. There is something wonderful, almost mystical, in my being the only one out upon this moonlit Sea of Japan. I feel the boat settle into its rhythm as I keep it on course for the very special place that I feel I must visit, a little haven of tranquility that I like to call waterfall cove.

Like the boathouse, the old boat has been patched up many times over the years, but it remains strong, sits well in the water and handles easily. My grandfather said that this was because it was originally built all those years ago by a master boat builder, and so like any finely made instrument, it has improved with age and the tender loving care given to it by my family over the years.

Sitting well down in the stern with my hand resting on the rudder, I feel the cold sea breeze on my face as the boat glides through the sea, the feel of the waves vibrating up through its keel. As a child, my grandfather would sit me down here in the stern on his fishing trips. In those days the boat felt huge, with its oak timbers towering up either side of me like great strong wooden walls.

I was never afraid in this old boat. Even now, when I have lost so much to the sea, I still have this feeling that the boat is protecting me from the dangers of the ocean. I feel the ebb tide take hold of the boat, pulling me out into the deep, and I turn into it as I need to take her well out to pull clear of the rocks before heading north up the coast.

Our family are direct descendants of the Ainu, the original people of Hokkaido, and we have fished these waters for centuries. The sea is our way of life, but sadly all too often it is also our way of death. My grandfather and I were the last of our family, my mother having died giving birth to me. My father, like so many Ainu fishermen, was lost at sea while I was still an infant. So, it was left to my grandfather, Yohji, to bring me up and to pass on the skills of fishing to me.

Yohji taught me well and I know every inch of this old boat: every plank of oak, all its strengths and little weaknesses, what it is capable of and what would be asking too much of it in rough seas. When my grandfather died, the boat became my continuity with all my family who had gone before me. At moments like this I feel that this old boat and I are one, the personification of generations of lives spent at sea. Sadly, I have not been able to pass these skills on to Ame, as he has never been strong enough. I know that it would be too much for him and would break him.

In contrast, my grandfather was a very strong wiry man, with the kind of strength that comes through generations of fishermen. And yet, he was the gentlest and kindness man you could ever meet, with endless patience. I watched him making this rudder upon which my hands now rest when the original one had broken in a gale, his strong hands skillfully and patiently carving the beautiful curve of the wood and then making the joint fit perfectly. Now when I take the rudder it is like holding his great strong hand in mine, so I am never afraid.

I never saw him get angry with the sea, even when it seemed to fight against us and making headway seemed almost impossible. He had a ready smile, and those very gentle eyes would inspire me with such confidence in his ability to handle anything the sea could hurl against the boat.

I only ever saw his face darken whenever I would ask him to tell me about my parents. Then I would see a shadow come over him, and he would look away and quickly change the subject. Eventually I just stopped asking him, as it obviously caused him too much pain and sadness to speak about losing them so young.

The boat now carries me clear of the point and I trim the sail and take her up along the coast. As the years went by, my grandfather began to rely upon me more and more on our fishing trips, as that great strength of his began to weaken. I could feel his sense of loss at having to give up so many of the things he had been so proud of, but I also saw the pride in his eyes as he watched me handle the boat and bring in the nets full of fish.

Apart from the sea, Yohji's great love was for haiku, which he also passed on to me. That, at least, was something that his waning strength could not rob him of. In the long hours we spent at sea, I never tired of hearing him talk of his love of haiku, passed on from generation to generation along with our fishing skills.

He loved to talk about how haiku had its mysterious origins with the Zen monks, who still use haiku to train the young monks how to meditate upon the mysteries that lie beneath the physical world. In Yohji's eyes, every haiku master was like a Zen mystic.

'They speak of those things which lie beneath the surface, Taki-san,' he would say in hushed tones, leaning over the edge of the boat to dip his hand beneath the waves. 'Their words have to be kept clear and simple, to let us see what lies beneath the words, like the fish just beneath the water as we pull in the nets.'

Haiku was like an extra special inheritance which he passed on to me, and it has deepened over the years. I sometimes wonder if this love of haiku was passed on to me solely through Yohji, or has it now run deep in our family tradition for so long that we are born with it? In any event, I in my turn try to pass it on to Ame, but he has yet to express any deep love for it, although he does appear to enjoy listening to mine.

For me, part of the fascination with haiku is how it is possible to contain so much within three simple lines: the first line to introduce the subject; the second taking it deeper by developing the shasai, the essence; and the third taking it deeper still to suggest the makato, the spiritual aspect which cannot be stated, only hinted at.

I used to think that the three levels of haiku were similar to gazing out to sea, then actually getting into the water to experience it more fully, and then finally diving deep below the waves to find what cannot be seen on the surface. The sea for me was like a vast reservoir of haiku, which I could never empty even if I lived a thousand lives. But then my love of the sea died when someone very close to my heart was drowned. From that moment on, I began to regard it with a deep sense of mistrust, which is shared by many fishermen who have lost loved ones at sea.

When I was younger, while waiting for the fish to come into the nets, I would sometimes get out of the boat and happily float beside it, like floating on a beautiful sea of liquid haiku.

'Taki by name and Taki by nature,' Yohji would say, and splash my face with water. My name, of course, means waterfall.

Perhaps he was right, and water is indeed part of my nature, because I used to love the feel of it flowing over my body, like the elemental ki energy of life flowing all around me, restoring my life and setting my body free to twist and turn and dive into the blue depths to be one with the silver fish. But all that was before the sea so cruelly took Shusaku from me. After that, I never felt the same way about it again, and never again trusted myself to its depths.

Many Hokkaido fishermen choose not to learn how to swim. Perhaps it goes back to the old Shinto belief that the kami, the elemental spirits that live down there in the deep, will take our lives when they are angry with us. I never used to believe this, but after Shusaku drowned, I began to wonder if perhaps there might be some truth in this old Shinto belief. While the Sea of Japan can be so calm and beautiful, it can turn quickly into a destructive force that shows no mercy.

Near the end of his life, my grandfather Yohji could do little more than rest in the stern with a blanket wrapped around him, trusting himself to the skills he had passed on to me as I took our boat out to sea. It was as though he was now the child and we had exchanged places. Our lives here, fishing on the rugged west coast of Hokkaido, are hard and often short; perhaps that is why we try to live them to the full before it is time to leave this beautiful place.

On our last trip together, he said that he wanted to take me to a very special place where he had never taken me before: the little cove where I am now headed, which lies just beyond the next point. As I turn the boat inland, the sun comes up upon this most special place that has so many memories for me, so full of joy and sadness.

2

Within grey sea mist
drifting across the water
the sound of voices.
Taki

As I take the boat around the point and turn inland, I can almost hear my grandfather's voice still giving me directions from his place in the stern. 'Take her well past the rocks on the point, Taki-san. Now bring her around. Keep the sail up. Now turn into the wave and let it take you in.'

There are no hidden rocks, just a gentle slope of sand all the way up to the beach, so I let the boat run in and ground itself in the sand. Climbing over the side, the cold water catches my breath as I run in my bare feet up to the dry sand. The sunrise holds the promise of one of those fresh early spring days, and I close my eyes and delight in the breeze coming off the sea.

The cove is deserted as always, for it lies in a secluded part of the coast and is not easy to get to, except by boat. I smile as I look at my single set of wet footprints in the sand, reinforcing my sense of solitude in this beautiful place. The cove is quite small, half-moon shaped with high rocks hiding it from view. From high up in the rocks, a small waterfall cascades down onto the golden sand and creates a small winding stream down to the sea. This place could not be more perfect. Even on windy days the rocks form a natural wind break, but today there is only the gentle sea breeze and I soak up the atmosphere of this little haven of tranquility.

Making my way up to the rocks, I laugh and feel like a teenager again as I cup my hands under the little waterfall and taste the deliciously cool fresh water. Then I sit down in my special place with my back to the rocks and soak up the scene around me, the rising sun now glistening upon the sea like gold.

I smile as I remember Ame as a child, exploring all around this little cove. When I asked him what he was looking for, he looked at me very seriously.

'The treasure,' he said. 'There must be treasure hidden in a place like this.'

He never did find the buried treasure that he was looking for, but only because he was looking in the wrong places. There is indeed a treasure to be found here, but it is a treasure beyond riches, a tranquility of soul that I have always found every time I come to this very special place.

On that very first visit here with my grandfather, I remember him watching me intently as I pulled in the sail and made the boat secure.

'It is beautiful here, Yohji-san,' I said. 'But why have you never brought me here before?'

'Come and sit here beside me for a moment, Taki-san,' he said, and once again I saw that dark shadow of sadness cross his face. 'I have brought you here today because I do not think that I will have the strength to do it again. And it is time that you knew the truth.'

'The truth?'

'The truth about your father, Kyoshi-san.'

As I sat down in the stern of the boat beside him, he put his arm around me and told me the secret that he had kept hidden from me all those years about my father's death.

'Your mother, Mariko-san, was quite small, just like you,' he said. 'Your birth was difficult and things went wrong inside. After she gave birth to you, it became quite obvious that she was dying. Your father held you up to her and your mother held you in her arms and kissed you. Then she handed you back to your father and said, "Her name is Taki-san."

'In a few moments she was gone, Taki-san. Your father stood there in total silence with you still in his arms. Then I noticed that you had also stopped breathing, Taki-san. We had to pull you from his arms as the tears fell down his face. Then he turned away, walked out, and got into the boat.

'I let him go, for he needed to be alone. But the old midwife who brought you into the world refused to let you die. She started rubbing you all over, then started breathing life into your mouth and pressing it down into your chest. I tried to stop her, but she would not let you go. And then, Taki-san, you started to breathe again. She saved your life.'

'And my father?' I managed to ask after a long silence as I let this all sink in. 'What about him?'

'When he did not return, we started a search. It was three days before we found the boat abandoned here, but he was never found. We believe that he died of a broken heart and that he walked into the sea. But they both held you in their arms, Taki-san. They both loved you very much.'

I remember sitting there in stunned silence with my grandfather's arms around me, trying to imagine my father's last hours in this place.

'Why did he come here?' I asked finally.

'This was their special place, Taki-san,' Yohji said. 'They both loved it here and would often come here to be alone. And I think that is why your mother called you Taki-san, waterfall,' he said, pointing to the waterfall flowing down from the rocks. 'I don't have very much to leave you, Taki-san,' he said. 'But I leave you this special place, and this,' he said, pointing to the old haiku that had been carved a long time ago into the stern of the boat.

Looking out to sea
grey clouds in darkening skies
lost in the mist.

'I found this haiku on the day we found the boat,' Yohji said. 'Your father must have carved it. It tells us something of the depth of his sense of loss for your mother. I think that he lost himself in the mist, to go and be with her, Taki-san.'

I had grown up with this old haiku carved into our boat, and never really gave it a second thought; it was just something that was part of the boat. But now my eyes are drawn to it every time I step aboard. It is full of depth and meaning, an insight into my father's love for my mother, a little touchstone to unite me with the two people who gave me life and who named me Taki-san after this little waterfall where I now sit.

Yohji and I spent most of that day in this cove, then he said that he was tired and asked me to take him home to the boathouse. On the way back the weather took a turn for the worse, with dark clouds and strong winds whipping up the tide. As I made our way back, I kept an eye on him, wrapped in his blanket asleep in the stern. He looked so small and vulnerable compared to the strong man who had once been in such complete control of this old boat and who had been my mentor all through life.

When we finally made it back to the boathouse, I tied the boat up then went back to help him up, but he was gone. I just sat down beside him with my arms around him for a very long time, this strong and very gentle man who had cared for me since the day I was born and who had taught me everything I know. And now, at the very end, he had taught me the truth about my parents, a parting gift to me, of who I am.

Now whenever I come to this beautiful place, I remember both him and my father and mother. I feel very close to them here. I imagine them young and happy, sitting here by the waterfall, drinking the cool fresh water and laughing. Life is often short here, and often sad, but we are surrounded by so much beauty. I now believe that my grandfather's death was actually quite beautiful too, falling asleep at sea in the old boat that he had loved and spent his life in.

The day after his death, I took our boat out as we had always done well before dawn, with our storm lamp looped over the mast. It was my way of keeping him close. As the coast faded away in the distance, I began to make out the lights of the storm lamps of the other fishing boats heading out also. Then I noticed how they were all following me at a respectful distance to honour Yohji-san. It was quite beautiful and my grandfather would have loved it.

In Hokkaido, we keep the traditional matsuri blessing ceremony every year to pray for good fortune and to remember those who have been lost at sea. Then we send little paper boats out on the tide with little lights in them. For me, watching the storm lamps on the real fishing boats was like a personal matsuri ceremony just for him.

3

Falling through the air
flowing down glistening rocks
sparkling waterfall.
Taki

Sitting here watching the sunlight sparkling in the waterfall, like a fountain of life, I feel as though my father and mother's tamashi are speaking to me through the water, their spirit reaching out to mine in this beautiful place, which they loved so much they named me after it.

It is like they had left me a legacy of this place, knowing that one day I would sit here by their waterfall and be close to them. I can almost hear their voices in the water falling onto the rocks, touch them in the cool spray of the waterfall on my face, kiss them in the fragrant zest of this sparkling pure essence of Hokkaido I taste on my lips.

Taking a slow walk along the length of the beach, I let the bittersweet memories flow back: of long hot summer days here with Ame playing in the sand and splashing in the water, of watching the deep blue tide washing away our footprints in the sand, of thinking of my father's footprints as he walked into the sea to be with my mother.

Then I think of my parent's happy times here, when they came here to be alone. Holding hands and walking along the beach, sitting by the waterfall, their words of love, watching the moon rise over the ocean. There is a beautiful timelessness about this place and as always, I have stayed longer than I intended.

I never find it easy to leave this place, but the sun is now casting longer shadows of the boat onto the sand, a gentle reminder that time is passing and I have yet another very special place to visit before the day is over. I say a prayer for my parents and thank them for their beautiful legacy of life, then I reluctantly turn my back on the waterfall and make my way back down the beach.

The tide has come up the beach a little way, so it does not take too much of an effort to push the boat out from the sand. As I get in and push away with the oars, I keep my eyes on the waterfall, like an old friend that I am reluctant to leave. Then I unfurl the sail and let it catch the breeze to take me back out to sea. The sail, like the boathouse, has been patched up so many times over the years that there is little of the original left. But even if I had the money, which I don't, I would not replace it with a new one. It is like a patchwork of our family history, each little square a flag of remembrance for those who sailed this old boat before me.

With my arm resting on the rudder, I let my eyes fall on my father's haiku. I see this as yet another legacy that has been waiting all these years for the right time for me to discover it and to understand the depth of his love. A love that could not bear to live without my mother; a legacy that has deepened my love of haiku even more, as it bonds me to the parents I never knew.

After my grandfather's death, I felt so utterly alone for he had been my constant companion. Now even the boathouse seemed so empty and soulless without him. Even taking the boat out failed to lift my spirits – I found myself just sitting in the stern with the boat still moored to the jetty, thinking of my grandfather and then of my father, while I ran my fingers over his final haiku carved into the wood. I also felt the need to somehow express the depth of my feeling in haiku, these little three line poems which say so much and have become such a depth of consolation to me.

As a special gift when I turned fifteen, my grandfather gave me a beautiful little brown leather notebook for me to write my haiku in. When you turn it on its side you see a beautiful golden butterfly etched onto the paper in gold leaf. I find it delightful that each page has a tiny piece of gold leaf on its edge, which is almost invisible, but when you close the book and fan the pages it is as though the butterfly spreads its wings in flight.

I had always intended to transfer all my haiku into it in my best writing, but never actually got round to doing it. In honour of my father's final haiku carved into our boat, I wrote my first haiku in the golden butterfly book in that moment.

Carved into oak wood
like words engraved in the heart
a haiku of love.
Taki

And so, haiku became my only source of solace whenever I took the boat out to sea, or when I was alone in the evenings in the boathouse. I found haiku all around me in the old boathouse, little things triggering memories of the things Yohji-san and I shared together and through this I began to feel a sense of healing.

Sometimes when I open the drawer of my tebaru to go through my haiku, I notice that my collection has been disturbed by Ame. Although he never writes haiku, he likes to listen to mine. I suspect that he also loves reading them when he is alone. I would love for him to become a haiku poet also, and I truly believe that he would discover that he too has inherited this gift that seems to run through our family.

He definitely has a creative spirit and his haikai drawings are truly delightful. With only a few lines he can capture a wave at sea, or a boat on the horizon. His talent speaks of a depth of sensitivity which could easily transfer over into writing. Perhaps when the time is right, he will discover this for himself.

We are so very close, having only each other for company. I know that he will be sitting on the porch right now looking out to sea, looking for signs of my returning. I feel a pang of guilt at causing him to worry about me, by not telling him where I was going. It would have been too hard to explain to him how I felt the need to go to our waterfall cove alone, just this once. It is such a special place for both of us, so full of happy memories of our many trips there over the years. But this is something that I really feel I had to do alone.

As I take the boat around the point and lose sight of the cove, I turn my mind to the other very special place that I must visit. It is not nearly as beautiful as the cove, little more than two outcrops of rock sticking up from the sea and bound together with an ancient rope, but to me it is the most special place in the world. In the old Japanese Shinto tradition of meoto-iwa, the rope signifies how these two rocks appear to be in such harmony with each other that their tamashi, their elemental spirit, are bound together, sharing one destiny.

Shusaku-san and I were childhood friends. His house was just along the beach from the boathouse and his father and my grandfather often helped each other with their catch of fish. I suppose it was inevitable that we would become friends, as both men took us out to sea to learn the ropes from childhood. When our boats drew near to each other, Shusaku would stand at the bough of their boat and shout my name into the wind, and I would laugh at his foolishness, but loved him for it really.

When we were not out fishing, we would often meet up and play on the beach with old bits of driftwood or anything we could find. I suppose our friendship became something deeper the day that he gave me a very beautiful shell that he picked up in the surf. Looking back, it was nothing much, but at the time I thought it was something very precious, which of course it became later, when we actually fell in love.

Our simple friendship gradually developed into that difficult adolescent stage, where we would get into arguments over silly things and go for days without talking. One day after such an argument, Shusaku really hurt me when he asked for his shell back, which I of course just threw at his feet and stormed off.

It was over a week before he came to the boathouse to say that he was sorry. I wasn't quite ready to forgive him and told him so. But then, without saying a word, he opened my hand and put my shell in it. When I looked, I saw that he had carved 'Taki-san' in the most beautiful tiny writing on the pearly inside of the shell. Looking back, I now think that was the moment when we actually fell in love.

When my grandfather died, our relationship developed into something more than teenage love. By then he was seventeen, a year older than me, with his own old secondhand fishing boat that his father had bought for him. I was by now sailing my boat single-handed. After a day's fishing, we fell into the habit of always holding back a little to let the other boats pull ahead, then we would pull our boats over to the two rocks to spend some time together, making it our secret place.

It was on one of these occasions that Shusako literally bound our love together.

'Throw me your rope, Taki-san,' he called, as we drew alongside the two rocks.

'Why?' I called back, for we had always simply tied our own ropes to the big ancient meoto-iwa rope that bound the rocks together.

'Just throw me your rope and you will find out,' he said.

I laughed at his foolishness and threw him my rope, then watched as he tied our two boat-ropes together in a sailor's knot and wound them both through the meoto-iwa.

'There,' he said, stepping over into my boat and putting his arm around me.

'There what?' I laughed.

'Now we are bound together for eternity, just like the two rocks.' Then he kissed me.

A simple little thing in itself, but it touched my heart and I shall never forget it. We never got the chance to get married properly, as the sea took him from me shortly after that. So, I look on that as our wedding day, and the two rocks where I am now heading as our very special place of love.

4

Under a night sky
deep rhythm of the sea
in the falling rain.
Taki

From out of the sea haze, I now catch sight of the two rocks and take the boat out a little to bring her in from seaward with the tide. Lowering the sail, I let the slow tide drift the boat in until it bumps gently against the rocks, then I loop my rope around the meoto-iwa rope.

The meoto-iwa is very strong and thick, made out of one continuous double loop to symbolise eternity. For me, it also conveys a sense of timeless security in a shifting sea, and it became like an emotional life-raft to cling to when the sea took Shusako-san away from me.

I sit down quietly in the stern and listen to the lapping of the tide against the rocks, letting the memories flow back, hearing Shusaku's whispers of love in my ear once more, remembering that night which changed our lives forever.

Once again, we had held our boats back from the rest of the fishing boats heading home in the evening, then we tied our boats together at the two rocks to be alone. We watched the sunset sink into the sea, then watched the moon rise gracefully into the night sky, turning the sea silvery blue. As we lay there in the stern of the boat, gazing up into an eternity of stars, it seemed like the most natural thing in the world that we kissed.

We had kissed before in a shy playful way, like teenagers on a date, and then that special shy kiss when Shusaku had bound our two ropes together, but this was something very different. This time when we kissed, we felt our souls meet and touch each other, until the world around us melted away and there was only his lips upon mine. We kissed as though we were the only two people in the world. We kissed as though this moment had been created just for us. We kissed until we became completely one, with my body melting into his and his body melting into mine.

Afterwards we lay in each other's arms in the soft and gentle warmth of love, listening to our breath, feeling our heartbeats, feeling the gentle rhythm of the sea rocking our boat. Then, a gentle warm rain began to fall and Shusaku covered us both with his coat. As we lay there listening to the rain, I let the tears fall freely down my face for this moment was amari ni utsukushi, too beautiful.

It was late when we finally got back to shore and tied our boats up for the night, risking one final shy kiss to say goodnight. I could not sleep, for my heart was too full of love. I lay there watching the moonlight cast its blue shadows on my window as I listened to the sea, remembering our moment of love.

I must have finally fallen asleep, because the wind awakened me, blowing hard against the boathouse, making the boat rock loudly against its mooring. By the time I got dressed and had some breakfast, the wind had grown stronger and I feared that we may be in for a storm. But I could not wait to see Shusaku, so I wrapped up well and took the boat along to the fishing harbour. The sea was getting even rougher as I guided the boat into the harbour and tied her up. I saw Shusaku talking to some other fishermen, but when he saw me, he waved and came over.

'They are trying to decide if it is going to be too rough to go out,' he said. And then, in a quieter voice, 'How are you, Taki-san?'

'In love,' I replied, and saw him smile.

'Me too,' he whispered, holding my gaze with those incredibly soft gentle eyes.

'Should we go out?' I asked as a strong gust of wind made me grab on to his arm.

'I think they want to risk it,' he said. 'The fishing has not been good as you know, and they need the money.'

'I'm not so sure, Shusaku-san. This looks as though it's going to get worse.'

'I'll be alright,' he said, taking my hand in his. 'But I think you should stay at home.'

'I'm as good as you,' I replied, giving him a playful push.

'Of course you are. Probably even better, in good weather,' he said, frowning. 'But you are right, this could get rough out there. I'll fish better if I'm not keeping an eye on you, little one.'

'Alright, just this once,' I said. I could see that he was really worried about me. 'But you promise not to take any chances out there. I mean it, Shusaku-san!'

'I promise,' he said, giving me a hug. 'And we share the catch fifty-fifty. Deal?'

'Deal,' I replied. We laughed and shook hands.

He cast a quick glance over to check if anyone was watching, then gave me a little kiss on my forehead. Then he jumped down into his boat to prepare to get underway.

I watched the boats head out into the rough sea, returning Shusaku's wave to me. I stood by the harbour watching them, until only their storm lamps could be seen, and then they too were lost in the darkness. Then I got back into the boat and took it back to the boathouse, tying it up fore and aft with double knots against the strengthening waves.

I spent the day doing odd jobs around the boathouse, keeping an eye out to sea and watching the weather as it continued to deteriorate. By late afternoon, the waves were crashing over the side of my boat as the storm got even worse.

With a sigh of relief, I finally saw the boats returning, being tossed around in the grey sea with the light fading. But as they drew nearer, a cold feeling began to creep inside me as I could not make out Shusaku's boat among them. I grabbed my coat and ran along the beach to the harbour in time to see them all coming in and tying up.

As the fishermen started to come ashore, I could tell that something was wrong by their expression.

'Where is Shusaku?' I asked one of the fishermen as he tried to walk past me.

My fear grew worse as he tried to walk on without replying, avoiding my eyes.

'Where is Shusaku?' I demanded, desperately grabbing his arm.

He tried to pull away, but I held him all the stronger, forcing him to meet my eyes.

'He turned back to try and help one of the boats that lost their sail and was being swept away in the storm,' he replied finally. 'Shusaku turned his boat into the storm and went after him. Then we lost sight of them both in the rough weather. They have probably been driven further down the coast. They will wait it out until the storm dies. Don't worry Taki-san, he is a good sailor, one of the best. He will be fine.'

Something in his eyes, however, betrayed his reassuring words, and I felt a cold hand clutch my heart. That cold fear stayed inside me as I walked home in the storm and sat by the window of the boathouse, watching and praying for his safe return.

The storm lasted well into the night. By the following morning the sky was still grey, but the storm had died and the sea was calm again. I could not eat or drink; I just sat there by the window all day looking for the first sign of his boat.

By the end of that day, I think I knew that Shusaku would not return, that he was gone. I lied to myself that his boat must have been blown a long way down the coast, perhaps even badly damaged, and he was walking back along the coast. I would then hear him knocking on the door of the boathouse and fall into his arms.

After three of the most terrible days of my life, sitting by the window desperately looking out to sea, I finally let the tears fall and the lies drop. He had gone. In my grief, I started to blame myself for his death. If only I had gone with him, he would never have left me to go and help the other boat.

With these thoughts and feelings haunting my every moment, I finally had to attend the matsuri ceremony for Shusaku and the other fisherman he had tried to save. But all the prayers in the world could not bring me any consolation. If only I had gone with him, then at least we might have died together, better that than this living nightmare without him.

Even the boathouse appeared grey and devoid of life, as though reflecting my state of mourning. Everything which had brought me so much comfort now seemed so empty as I sat there alone in my grief. My only source of consolation, which was not really consolation at all, was the shell that Shusaku-san had given me with my name written upon it. Sometimes I held it very gently, remembering our happy childhood days; at other times I gripped it so hard in my grief that it almost made my hand bleed.

It was then I knew that terrible feeling which had driven my father to walk into the sea to be with mother, for this was not living, it was a living death. I looked out to sea with my eyes full of hatred, for it had taken Shusako-san's life, all I wanted to do was to walk out there to be with him.

5

At one in the night
the sound of two hearts beating
in the falling rain.
Taki

In time, the searing pain of my grief very slowly gave way to something even worse. An utter emptiness overwhelmed me, leaving me devoid of all sense of feeling, as though draining my life from me. Going on solitary walks along the beach, feeling the wind in my face, listening to the cries of the seabirds, all the things that used to bring me joy, now became intolerable reminders of my isolation. Even the boathouse, which had always been a haven of consolation, now appeared empty and soulless as I lay awake each night staring out of my window into a dark empty sky.

And so I lived, or rather existed, with no thought for food or drink. When the consolation of sleep allowed me to forget, I would awake once again to the living nightmare. As I walked along the beach my eyes constantly turned seaward, in the vain hope of catching sight of Shusaku's boat. At night I would burn the driftwood I had found on my solitary walks, watching the flames flicker dark shadows all around the boathouse. Then, when the fire died out, the darkness seemed to envelope me, compounding my utter isolation.

From somewhere inside, I drew the strength to endure the unendurable and slowly, terribly slowly, I learned to face my life once again alone. Out of sheer necessity, I had to force myself back into the boat and took her out to lay the nets down for a catch, quite simply to survive.

As I sailed past the two rocks, it was as though my heart was being torn from within me and I forced myself to look away and keep sailing on. Beyond the two rocks, the ocean floor falls sharply away and the tide grips the boat in a different way, making me aware of the depth of the ocean under the keel of the boat. For me, it was like a somber reminder of the malignant power that had pulled Shusaku down there into its depths.

As I lowered the net down into the water and sat down in the stern to let the boat drift with the tide, my eyes fell on the haiku that my father had carved into the stern, feeling the depth of that pain that had made him walk into the sea. Then as I sat there, a terrible temptation came over me to do the same. Just one step over the side and I would be with Shusaku in the deep. It was as though the sea that had taken Shusaku was now silently tempting me to join him.

Something stopped me ending it all there. I'm not sure what, but I found myself quickly pulling in the net and turning the boat back to shore. I had not been out long enough to catch very much, but it was enough to keep me going for a few days, keeping a few for myself and selling the rest to Saito, the fishmonger.

When I docked the boat in the harbour and presented Saito with the boxes of fish, as usual he tried to undercut the price. I was in no state to haggle over money and simply nodded my head, took the money from his horrible sweaty little hands and took the boat back along the coast for home. At least I now had enough money to supplement my fish with some rice and vegetables.

When I tied the boat up back at the boathouse, I collapsed onto my tatami, totally exhausted emotionally and physically as I had hardly eaten or slept properly for a very long time. But with some sense of achievement, I let myself fall asleep. When I awoke some time later, I actually felt a little hungry and cooked some of the fish on the stove, savouring the aroma as I grilled it over the crackling driftwood.

I ate the fish by the window as I watched the sun go down. It was only now, in the safety of the boathouse, that I let my mind dwell on the terrible temptation I had felt out there. The sea had been one of the abiding joys of my life until it took Shusaku, and now it was tempting me to join him. From that day on, every time I got into the boat I became aware of a deep distrust of the sea, especially when I had to take the boat out into the deep water beyond the two rocks.

And so, my life settled into a pattern of solitude: taking the boat out only when necessary to catch enough fish to survive, going for walks in search of driftwood, cooking my meals by the stove, and finally falling asleep on my tatami looking out of my window at the night sky. The one thing that I still could not bear to do was visit our special place, where we had made love that night before Shusaku died. It was like a wound that had never healed and was too painful to touch.

One dark overcast night, as I sat by the window looking out to sea, that terrible temptation returned. I realised why I had not been able to go to the two rocks: deep in my heart I knew that if I did, then I would not return, but join him out there in the deep. I realised that all my hard work of late was simply a means of denying what I really wanted to do, which was to walk into the sea to be with Shusaku.

It was as though the sea was whispering this into my ear with every sound of the waves playing against the boat tied up to the jetty. I stood up and steadied myself with my hands upon the little tebaru by the window, feeling my legs go very weak at the thought of what I was now actually going to do, for I could no longer fight the temptation. But then, in that dreadful moment, a gentle rain began to fall, softly in the night. I watched it fall into the sea and I heard it upon the roof of the boathouse.

In my grief, I had forgotten just how beautiful the rain could be. The temptation left me; I knew that I still wanted to live and that Shusaku would want me to live, to experience all these beautiful moments that had been taken from him.

I lay down on my tatami and closed my eyes, listening to the rain in the night whispering in my ear like a lover. In that moment, I felt my child's heartbeat within me, and the tears fell freely down my face. I was not alone, and Shusaku was still very much alive and with me in the child we had created that night. And so, I named my child Ame, rain, for he came to me in that gentle rain that taught me how to live again.

In Japan, we believe that each of us have to find our own unique ikigai, our reason for living. I had now found mine in the child that Shusaku had left me. As I lay there listening to the rain in perfect stillness, feeling my child's life within me, a haiku began to take form in my heart to celebrate this special moment for eternity.

At one in the night
the sound of two hearts beating
in the falling rain.

Is it the poet who creates such haiku? Or is it the haiku moment that creates the poet, filling the mind with such inspiring beauty that they feel compelled to capture it in writing?

I awoke the next morning to sunshine flooding into the boathouse and lay there intensely happy to be alive, my hands resting upon the baby in my womb, listening to the sound of my breath and imagining it flowing inside to fill my child with life.

I smiled as I began to realise that I was actually very hungry, and got up and cooked some more fish for breakfast, delighting in the taste as though for the very first time. From my window the sea was a perfect blue, with hardly a ripple against the boat, and I knew exactly what I wanted to do.

I hurriedly got dressed and into the boat. There, with just enough breeze to get underway, I took her out along the coast and headed toward waterfall cove. I wanted to feel close to my parents in their special place, to celebrate the fact that with the life they had given to me, I had now created a new life.

When I turned the boat into the cove, it was every bit as beautiful as the first time. Remembering my grandfather's instruction, I let the sail take her well up the sandy beach, then stepped over the side to feel the deliciously cool water on my feet, then the feel of the warm soft sand as I made my way up the beach toward the waterfall, glistening in the clear sunlight.

In a moment of pure joy, I put my hands into the waterfall and tasted this cool essence of life, then laughing as I sprinkled it on my face and sat down with my back against the rocks, lifting my face to the sun. Over the years I have returned to this very special place in which my soul delights, but I always remember this visit in which I felt that I had started to live again and to delight in life. I spent the whole day there, just sitting listening to the sound of the waterfall. Our life here is so beautiful and vulnerable, like the cherry blossom in springtime, and all the more precious for that.

When I finally sailed the boat out of the cove, I took her back along the coast. As the sun began to set, I pulled the boat over by the two rocks, where Shusaku and I had made love. I felt that I needed to bring our child here and to be close to Shusaku again. As waterfall cove was my parents' special place, this was our special place. I felt that I could now come here any time to be close to Shusaku, and one day I would bring our child out here and tell him all about the father he never knew.

6

Fishing boats at sea
white sails on the horizon
drifting in the breeze.
Taki

Ame was born premature and quite tiny, but he had Shusaku's fine features and lots of dark hair even then. The sheer joy that Ame brought to me was something that I had never experienced before, a deeper kind of love, perhaps even deeper than my love for his father. This very tiny and fragile human being clung to my breast to be fed and kept safe and warm, instinctively wrapping his arms around my neck whenever I picked him up, his tiny hands wrapping around my finger, not wanting to ever let go.

This was a love that went beyond self and yet I saw myself in him as we lay on our tatami with me perfectly happy, just endlessly looking at his face up close to mine. It was during one of these moments that the thought occurred to me: this consolation that Ame had brought to me in my loss of Shusaku was not only meant for me, but would bring consolation to Shusaku's parents also, knowing that they had a grandson.

His mother had never been very friendly toward me and I somehow got the feeling that she felt I was not good enough for her son. However, I felt that despite all that, we now had a mutual bond through Ame, which should be shared.

Summoning up my courage, I wrapped Ame up in warm blankets and walked along the beach to Shusaku's parents' house. It was midday and I knew that Shusaku's father would be out at sea. As I walked along the beach, I tried to think of what I was going to say, but everything I tried seemed somehow to come out wrong. And so, arriving at their house, I took a big deep breath and knocked on the door, trusting that the right words would come.

When Shusaku's mother opened the door, I was shocked at how much she had aged from Shusaku's death. Her face had become deeply lined, her hair almost totally grey, and her eyes were like the eyes of a very old woman. It was those incredibly old and empty eyes that held mine and robbed me of any words. And then the eyes turned toward Ame, and I instinctively drew him closer to my breast because of the look of anger she gave both me and my child. Then, without a single word, she turned her back upon me and closed the door.

I stood there looking at the wood of the door, totally stunned by this expression of anger, which almost bordered on hatred. I felt condemnation in those hard eyes, as though Shusaku's death was somehow my fault. With all the joy Ame had brought to me now totally drained out of me, I turned away and made my way home.

By the time I got back to the boathouse, my shock at Shusaku's mother's reaction to her grandson had turned to sorrow, sorrow for her, because I knew more than anyone the depth of her grief at Shusaku's death. But there was nothing I could do, for even looking at his child had only seemed to make her pain and anger at his death even worse.

I awoke early the next morning with the sound of heavy rain beating down on the roof of the boathouse and lay there in the warmth of our tatami, with Ame held in my arms. Then, I heard footsteps coming along the porch and stopping at the door. Wrapping Ame up in the tatami, I went over and slid open the door to see Shusaku's mother standing there in the pouring rain. With tears rolling down her face, she just stood there in total silence, her grief clearly beyond words.

There was nothing I could say; it was not a time for words. I simply held her in my arms, the two of us standing in the rain, feeling the terrible pain that united us and bonded us together. Then I took her by the hand into the house and placed Ame in her arms. Watching her hold my son to her breast, I somehow knew that she was remembering holding Shusaku like that when he was an infant. Now at least she had the consolation of holding his son in her arms also.

I had lost Shusaku, but the thought of losing Ame one day to the sea would be completely unbearable and leave me as totally broken as Shusaku's mother. I think it was in that moment that I resolved never to let my son out of my sight for a moment whenever we put to sea.

In those early years, I had to wrap Ame up warm and take him out in the boat with me to earn a living. I found the local fishermen very kind and compassionate toward me. In our naivety, Shusaku and I had thought our little rendezvous at the two rocks was our secret, but of course the fishermen must have known, as they knew now that Shusaku was Ame's father. They said little to me but always gave me a warm smile and would help me land the boxes of fish on to the jetty for Saito the fishmonger, greedy as ever to undercut the prices.

Saito probably saw me as an easy opportunity to swindle. What was even more horrible was the sly lecherous look he gave me when he put the money into my hands, letting his hands linger on mine until I pulled away. It was obvious that he saw me as an easy opportunity in that way as well. However, I never even tried to hide the loathing I felt for him and I think that is why he began to hate me.

Then as time went by, I began to notice how even the fishermen's attitude began to change toward me. They started to avoid me and no longer helped me to land my catch on to the jetty. I had grown up with these people, who were friends of my grandfather. I could not understand why they hardly even spoke to me anymore. Eventually, I found out from an old friend of my grandfather that a rumor had started to spread among the fishermen that I was un no waru, unlucky.

'What is this nonsense all about?' I demanded.

'They say it is because Yohji died with you in the boat with him,' he replied, 'and Shusako died after you and he had spent time together in your boat. So, they say that you and your boat are unlucky. So sorry, Taki-san.'

'And who is it that is spreading this nonsense?' I demanded angrily.

The old fisherman shrugged his shoulders and did not reply, but I got the impression that he did know but did not want to say. Nevertheless, I already instinctively felt that I knew who was behind the ugly rumor and I stormed on to the jetty, where I found Saito sitting in his usual place.

'Is it you that started this ridiculous rumor about me being un no waru?' I demanded.

In reply, he merely shrugged his shoulders and fixed me with that sly lecherous look in his eyes, which was all the proof I needed. I was filled with such white-hot anger that I almost hit him as I stood there glaring at him with my fists clenched tight at my sides. I think that if he had said a single word to me then I would have attacked him, but he just sat there, obviously enjoying my frustration. With an extreme effort of will, I gave him a look of total contempt and stormed off.

I was so angry, not only at Saito, but more so at the fishermen whom I thought were my friends. How could they believe such vile nonsense? I swore to have nothing more to do with any of them and for days I did not even take the boat out to sea. But then, as I cooled down a little, I realised that I had a son to care for and so of necessity I had to swallow my pride and start fishing again. I made a point of keeping my boat well away from the rest of the boats to show them that I wanted nothing more to do with them.

As the days wore on, however, I grudgingly began to accept that they were only acting out of superstitious fear. The sea can take any of us at any time, and these good and simple men had their own families to worry about. No, it was Saito alone who was to blame for my being stigmatised and left feeling even more isolated.

The hardest thing of all was that I had to swallow my pride for my son's sake and take my catch of fish to Saito at the end of the day. I deliberately left the fishing grounds before the others and was the first to tie up on the jetty. It took all of my self-control to put my few boxes of fish on his table for payment.

The sly look he gave me turned my stomach, but I stood there with as much dignity as I could muster and looked him straight in the eye. Casting a scornful look at my catch, he then threw the money on to the table, half of what it was worth.

'What do you call that?' I said.

'That's all it's worth to me,' he sneered. 'Take it or leave it.'

We both knew that I had no choice but to take it, as he was the only fishmonger. Once again, I had to swallow my pride and scoop up the money. But the die had now been cast and I would have to work twice as hard now to make ends meet.

What followed was years of hard work and long hours at sea, with my son wrapped up in the boat beside me. Hard as it was, I now look upon those days in a golden mist of joy, holding my son to my breast, feeling his heart beat against mine as our boat rocked him gently to sleep.

When it was time to take Ame to the priest, I began to fear what sort of reception Fr. Koji might give to me, an unmarried mother. But once again, I put my own pride aside for the sake of my son.

Our little Franciscan church sits on the hill overlooking the harbour, as though looking out for the fishing boats at sea. It's a small simple building in keeping with the style of our village, but inside the light streams in through large windows, making everything glow in the sunshine and even more in the moonlight. As a little girl, Yohji would bring me here, sometimes after a day's fishing, to light a candle and say a prayer in the soft light of the evening.

As I entered the church, my eyes fell on the row of small red akari candle holders, immediately taking me back to my childhood. Kneeling down, I put a coin in the slot and lit one of the little candles to say a prayer for Ame, wrapped up and fast asleep in my arms.

'Taki-san. Is that you?'

Fr. Koji had entered so silently that I had not heard him. He was very small and slightly built, even for a Japanese man, with a small white beard and short hair. His appearance was unchanged in the sixteen years that I had been coming to this church, which he kept immaculately clean all by himself.

The Franciscans had come to Japan eight hundred years ago, shortly after the Jesuits, but the simple working people took the Franciscans especially to their hearts because of the simplicity of their teaching that God is love, and the simplicity of their lives with little more than their brown habits tied together with a piece of rope. The Franciscan spirituality of seeing God within all things also blended in easily with Shinto's reverence of nature.

'Good morning, Fr. Koji,' I replied. 'I came to ask if you would baptise my son?' As I said this, I turned Ame round for the priest to see his face.

Fr. Koji was silent for a long moment, and I began to fear what he might say. But then he very gently took Ame from me and held him in his arms.

'And is your son to be called Shusaku, after his father?' he asked gently. He obviously knew all about the events of Shusaku's death and my having his son, but the gentle way in which he asked the question conveyed only compassion for me and for my loss.

'I would like him to be baptised Ame, father,' I replied.

'An unusual name, Taki-san,' he said, as Ame chose this very moment to waken and look up at him.

Then I told him about the night when I became aware of my son's life within me in the rain. Once again, the old priest became very quiet for a long moment as he thought this over.

'Then this will be the first time I have ever baptised rain,' he said smiling, and then turned to lead us over to the baptismal font.

And so, this perfectly gentle old priest poured the holy water over Ame's head and said the prayers, then handed him back to me. When I eventually thanked him and turned to leave, he told me to wait a moment, and then he went over and picked up the small red akari in which my candle for Ame was still burning.

'Take this home with you,' he said, putting his hand gently on my head. 'God is love, Taki-san. And if we live in love, we live in God. And God lives in us.'

That night I relit the small red akari and let it burn by the window as I held Ame in my arms, watching the moon play upon the water. In haiku, the words if they are chosen well, can have a profound effect upon people. The old priest had said those beautiful words to me just like a simple little three-line haiku, and they did what all good haiku do: they touched my soul.

I slept very peacefully that night, with the akari left burning and with Ame sleeping quietly in my arms. It did not matter to me anymore what the fishermen thought about me, or if Ame and I had to live our lives in solitude in the boathouse. So be it, for it would be a simple life lived in love.

7

Through the wind and rain
fishing boats heading for home
storm lamps in the night.
Taki

I feel now that it is time for me to go home. I have stayed out much longer than I had intended and Ame will by now be worried about me. But this really was something that I felt I had to do, just one last time. We never talk about it, but we both know how sick I have become.

A swell in the tide catches me unaware as I stand up to untie the rope from the rocks, and I lose my balance and fall back down again. As I look around me, I notice how rough the sea has become. I have stayed out too long and let myself become overtired, and that swell of the sea could have easily taken me over the side. The sea is starting to toss the boat from side to side, like some malignant force trying to unsettle me. Once again, I feel that deep mistrust of this ocean rising up within me, the ocean that took Shusaku from me.

With these feelings of unease building up inside me, I stand up again and untie the rope from the rocks, then unfurl the sail to get underway. It seems that the sea is determined not to let me go, as the wind quite suddenly dies away, leaving the sail hanging loosely to the mast and my boat becalmed. Then the sea itself is becalmed as the waves die away and the water around the boat becomes as still as a lake. I thought I had experienced all the mood swings which the Sea of Japan is known for, but I have never known anything quite like this.

It is as though the boat is resting upon a sea of glass, perfectly mirroring the night sky ablaze with stars as far as the horizon, where the sea and sky seem to meet and become one. Fascinated, I sit in silent awe of this quite majestic scene of breath-taking beauty.

All the feelings of enmity and mistrust of the sea that I had experienced only a moment ago now dissolve in the face of this display of natural, or rather supernatural, serenity. Like a little girl once again, I gaze all around me in fascination as the boat rests in this sea of moonlight. I know that this is probably the last time I will be able to take the boat out. It feels almost as though the sea is saying goodbye, by revealing the depth of her beauty to me.

I reach out over the side of the boat and touch the cool dark blue water, like friends feeling the need to shake hands after a quarrel. And then, in that moment of touch, I have the distinct feeling of Shusaku's presence. It feels as though within this moment of absolute stillness of the sea, he is reaching out to somehow let me know that all is well with him, as though his hand is touching mine in the sea. Tears of absolute joy flow down my face and I watch them fall into the water to be with him.

As I sit here in awed silence, I have the most profound feeling of being at one with everything. This majestic beauty which surrounds me feels as though it has become a part of me. The sea, the sky, the stars, and the very air which I breathe are part of me and I part of them, my tears dissolving in this beautiful blue water, which runs through my own veins and gives me life.

I feel at peace once again with my friend the sea and can now see beyond my loss of Shusaku that it is not some malignant kami that takes life at a whim. It is a most beautiful part of nature, and I can no more blame the sea for creating rough seas than I can blame the wind, or blame the moon for causing the tide to flow. And it is the same water that flows here in the deep that flows so beautifully at waterfall cove, or in the gentle rain after which I named my son Ame.

Then, as suddenly as it had come, the moment is gone as the sea breeze picks up again, the tide returns, and I am free to sail back home. This moment will live with me for however long I may have left to live in this beautiful place.

When the doctor told me that I was dying, it did not come as a total shock, as I had been growing increasingly aware for months that something was very wrong. Although I have always been quite small and thin, I have always been strong within myself. Undoubtedly the hard life I have led, however, must have taken its toll upon me. The winters can be very hard, with biting winds and nets which almost freeze as you haul them out of the sea. Working from before dawn to after dark, sometimes with little to show for it, and barely enough to live on.

This last winter has been particularly hard upon me and gradually I began to feel my strength weaken within me. At first, I tried to just work it off, but as the time went by I gradually had to admit that something was very wrong. After a lot of tests, the doctor finally informed me that I had leukemia and that it was too far advanced for any treatment. I have no fear of dying; it is as natural as being born.

In Japan we believe that the life force, the ki, flows around and within us, and eventually when it begins to flow out of us then our life comes naturally to its end. Whatever form our final illness takes, it is simply this life force leaving our body, as natural as the tide flowing in and then flowing back out to sea again.

My fear, however, was always for Ame. Without me, how would he survive on his own, being unable to take the boat out to fish? We have lived from day to day, and I leave him without any means of support. There is always this feeling deep within me that it is my fault he is so weak and vulnerable, because I was not able to carry him to full term in my womb.

Since the doctor told me that I was dying, I have been trying to find the right moment to tell Ame. We are so very close; I know that it will break his heart. And so, I have continued to try and pretend that everything is alright and carry on as usual, but I know that I cannot do this for much longer. Even tonight this short sail has almost drained all the energy out of me, and I feel the ki, the life force, continue to drain away from my body.

Perhaps it is because my ki energy is beginning to flow away from me, that I am increasingly conscious of it all around me here tonight. I feel it in the sea breeze that has now picked up again, and in the water that is once again splashing against my boat. And when this beautiful gift of living ki finally leaves my body, then I will leave this place and go to another, even more beautiful place. In that place beyond the sea, where I know that Shusaku-san waits for me. For in that beautiful moment, I truly felt his presence and I know that all is well. And now I find that my fear for how my son will cope after my death has also gone, for I have experienced such a serene presence within all this beauty here tonight that I now trust my son Ame into that divine care that holds all things in being.

When I have left this place, then I will tell Shusaku of the beautiful son which we created that last night we spent together, tell him that he has his father's fine features, tell him of his gentle and sensitive nature, tell him of how noble and serene he looks when he sits in zazen to draw his haikai pictures of the swans flying into the clouds. I will tell him of the very deep and sensitive way he has of looking at this majestic Sea of Japan by whose shores we live our short but beautiful lives.

8

Drifting through the mist
the call of swans in the bay
whispers of old friends.
Taki

As Ame grew, it soon became obvious that he would not be able earn a living as a fisherman. Despite all my efforts in helping him to take his first steps and all the daily massage and exercises, his legs remained very weak. Out here, on the Sea of Japan in rough weather, it would be impossible for him. But he loved being in the boat just as much as I did, and we delighted in our simple life together.

As a child he took particular delight in watching me let the nets down and then letting the boat drift with the tide. He would then lean over the side with his hand in the sea, feeling the flow of the water. At other times he would sit up in the bow with his eyes closed, feeling the sea breeze on his face, or sit lost in fascination over the mystery locked inside some old piece of driftwood he had found.

I became convinced that he would become a poet, drawing upon his delight in everything around him. As it turned out, his talent proved to be in capturing all these things in his haikai drawings, of fish swimming in the nets, or the waves around the boat, or the sea birds that followed us, swooping around our nets as we hauled in the fish.

When he got tired of whatever he was doing, he would sit beside me and play the haiku game, with me saying the first two lines and he having to come up with the third. But his heart was never in it, and I suspect he only did it to please me. After a few attempts, he would soon lose interest and return to his drawings. Then left on my own with all the time in the world, I would retreat into my own inner world where the real haiku live, letting my net down into that deep silent sea of the mind in search of haiku.

In the evening, when we had sold our catch, we would sit by our stove eating some of the fish we had brought home. Then he would show me his drawings and I would read him my haiku. And that was our life, simple but beautiful. We both took it hard when he became of age to go to school. I would take him there before setting out to sea on my own, being sure to return in time to bring him home again. Both of us were impatient for his days off so that we could set out to sea again together.

School was difficult for him and I am sure that he was often bullied, but he kept it all to himself. There is a quiet courage in Ame, the kind of courage that makes ordinary people face difficulties with dignity. I quite often found him looking quietly at my kintsukuroi picture on the wall above my tebaru. It is a photograph of a painting by an unnamed artist that I came across in an old magazine, of a broken pot that had been put together again by pouring molten gold into the cracks. The artist skillfully used subtle colours to make the gold shine against the dark colours of the pot. I fell in love with it and cut it out of the magazine. I know that Ame sees himself as broken, and I suspect that is why he is drawn to my kintsukuroi. Unfortunately, people are not as easily made whole as pots. If only we were.

We both gave one huge sigh of relief when his school days were finally over and he never had to return there. We put to sea the next morning to celebrate his freedom, delighting in the sea breeze, the swell of the tide, and the silver fish shimmering in the blue water as we hauled in the nets. But my eyes never left him for a moment all the time we were at sea, the old fear haunting me that somehow the sea in one of her cruel moods might take my son the way she had taken his father.

However, the sheer joy in Ame's face was a delight to watch, as he took up his place again at the bow with his drawing pad to capture the beauty that surrounded us. His natural talent had deepened over the years and it fascinated me to see how he could capture the images around us. In a few simple lines, he could show the ripples of a wave rising up in the bow of the boat, or a flock of birds taking to the air.

As he grew into adolescence, I began to see more of his father Shusaku in his features and mannerisms, particularly in his quiet gentleness. But there is a depth to Ame that is quite unique, a stillness within him when he is intent upon his drawing, or just sitting on the porch looking out over the sea. Perhaps it is a gift to make up for his frailty, or perhaps it is because of it.

Having never had the strength to run about as a child, he would content himself by just sitting still and being at one with his surroundings. Perhaps Ame's stillness is actually the molten gold that turns his brokenness into kintsukuroi. Of course, I could never say this to him. How could you suggest to a teenage boy that what he sees as brokenness has actually made him a more whole person?

Now I feel that it really is time for me to cast off from the two rocks and sail for home, where Ame is no doubt waiting anxiously for my return. It is only a short sail, but as I draw near the shore, I feel the energy draining from my body. It is my own fault and I know that I have stayed out far too long and overtired myself, but I would not have missed this experience for all the treasure in the world.

Then, as my strength continues to fail, I see a light from the shore. As I pull nearer I make out the figure of Ame, standing there on the porch holding the storm lamp to guide me home. My feelings of sheer exhaustion now mix with those of guilt, as I know that my son has most probably been standing there with that lamp since it became dark.

Through sheer weakness, I clumsily bump the boat hard against the jetty and sheepishly hand the rope up to Ame to tie it up. He doesn't say a word, just very gently takes my hand and helps me up, then takes my arm and helps me inside.

'I'm so sorry, Ame-san,' I say as he closes the door behind us. 'I just had to take the boat out.'

'Where did you go?' he asks, gently helping me out of my coat.

'I went to the cove.'

He looks at me for a long moment with those deep understanding eyes.

'I see,' he says finally. And I know that he does see. 'Rest now, Taki-san. I'll get you some tea.'

'I don't deserve you,' I say. He only smiles, but he cannot hide the concern in those very deep eyes.

By the time he has returned with the tea, I have recovered enough to get changed into a dry kimono, although I am still trembling with the cold. Sitting down beside the stove and sipping the hot tea with shaking hands, I tell him all about my sail.

'Everything was so perfect, Ame-san,' I say as I bring my story to an end. 'I'm only sorry that I stayed out so late. I hope you weren't worried, I was in no real danger.'

Ame just slowly shakes his head. He has a way of saying a lot without any words being spoken. 'You must rest, Taki-san,' he says finally as I drain the last of the tea. Then he helps me to stand up and walk over and almost collapse onto my tatami.

As I lay there listening to the sea outside, Ame lights our little akari lamp and I let my eyes rest upon its warm red light until they grow heavy. As then, as I say a silent prayer, I feel myself drifting off to sleep.

'What are you praying for, Taki-san?' Ame asks. He knows me so well, he even knows when I am praying.

'I'm praying for you,' I whisper back, then surrender to sleep.

I slept until dawn, drifting in and out of dreams about meeting Shusaku again at our secret rendezvous, about sitting by the waterfall all alone in the cove, about walking along the beach collecting driftwood with Ame as a little boy holding my hand again. Then, as I open my eyes, I smile as he is right there sitting on the floor beside my tatami.

'How are you feeling?' he asks.

'Better,' I lie, avoiding his eyes, for I still feel very weak.

'No more sailing today, Taki-san,' he says. 'I'll make us some tea.'

Outside my window, a grey mist hangs over the bay as I listen to the water gently lapping against the boat outside. We both sit in silence looking at the mist as we drink our tea. Silence for us is like an old friend who visits us often and we delight in its presence. And then, the silence is broken by one of the most beautiful sounds: swans flying in to rest in our bay on their spring migration north.

'Listen, Ame-san,' I whisper.

'I know,' he replies, peering out into the grey mist to try and catch sight of them coming in to land. Like a little boy once again.

I asked him once why he loved the swans so much. He took a long time to answer and then finally said that it was because they appeared out of the clouds, and then would disappear back into them again, their snow-white wings dissolving into the sky. For me, this was pure haiku and I told him so. But he just smiled at my efforts once again to try to convince him to write. However, he did shortly after this produce an exquisite haikai drawing of swans flying into clouds.

'I will be alright here,' I tell him, as I see his eyes wandering to the window. 'I know you want to sit out there with your swans.'

'You know me too well, Taki-san,' he said.

'I'm your mother,' I reply. 'Go on, out you go, I want to rest. And bring me back a haiku of the swans in the bay.'

He only smiles at my feeble attempt to make a haiku poet out of him. I hear him settle down on the porch outside my window, listening to his swans in the mist. He could be out there for hours, sitting in his silence and stillness. Was he born like this, or did this beautiful tranquil place make him like this? I have no regrets about our solitary lives in this bay. As I look around the old boathouse, every inch of it is full of precious memories. It is almost like an old and dear friend, which I will find hard to let go. But I know that I must, as I feel my life drawing to a close.

It takes all of my strength to get up from the tatami, and I have to hold on to the tebaru while I open the drawer to get out my book of haiku with the golden butterfly. Collapsing back on my bed, I leaf through the pages and relive all the precious haiku moments that I captured, the words bringing back vivid memories of my time here. They say that we come into this world with nothing and that we leave it with nothing. Perhaps so, but I like to think that I will take my haiku with me, for I found them in that deep sacred place of the soul, that place which does not die.

I close my eyes again and listen to the sound of the sea lapping against our old boat, as though whispering to me to come away again, to cast off and sail away once more. Then I hear the swans again, their call drifting across the sea, such a beautiful soulful sound.

I leave Ame with almost nothing. An old boat which he does not have the strength to sail, and an old ramshackle boathouse than can barely keep out the rain. But I also leave him with this exquisitely beautiful place and all the memories we have shared together. It is not true that we take nothing with us when we go, for we take the love we have known, for love also comes from that deep sacred place of the soul and does not die.

As I feel my life beginning to slip away moment by moment, Ame's name is on my lips to call him, but then I stop myself. For if I do, the pain and distress that he will not be able to hide will make my dying worse for both of us. So, I lay back and just listen to the swans and know that he is just outside my window, better this way. He will find me asleep, with my haiku in my hands, and he will know that I am at peace.

If Ame were to ask me once again what I was praying for, I would tell him I am praying that he will grow in love and that he will find peace within that quiet place where he goes when he becomes very still. And that he will find that special ikigai which is given to each of us to find.

I turn to a new page in my haiku book, to leave something special behind for him. Perhaps it will at last inspire him to begin to write all those beautiful haiku that I know are locked inside him. And from that deep and silent place where the haiku live inside me, I find what I am looking for.

A haiku about his swans, about their voices calling through the mist, about me going into that mist which hovers over the sea that I love. And then, I imagine that the voices are calling to me, whispering to me to come to them through the mist.

With my hands shaking as my strength fades, I write my final haiku to Ame.

Drifting through the mist
the call of swans in the bay
whispers of old friends.
Taki

I smile as I imagine him reading it over and over again as the years go by. Closing my eyes, I leave the book open in my hands and listen once again to the gentle sound of the sea against the boat. Listening to its whispers, whispering memories of me taking Ame out in the boat... of silver fish in shimmering blue water... of silver moonlight on the sea... of sailboats drifting off into the distance.

BOOK THREE

1

Moonlight in the trees
echoing through the shadows
the toll of a bell.
Shijin

A grey misty dawn drifts through my window as I close my eyes again to try and hold onto the dream before it sinks back down into the depths of my mind from where it came. Sail boats drifting over the horizon, but the more I try to hold onto the dream, the more it drifts away. With a sigh I let it go, then turn my mind to the comfort of my tatami, making the most of it before I have to get up.

As I lie reflecting on my dream, I wonder: what could it be about? Perhaps running out of time with my advancing years? The boats slipping over the horizon, like my time slipping away? Perhaps I will write a haiku today about the passing of time.

I brace myself against the cold and get up. Looking out of the window, I see that it has been snowing again in the night, covering everything in a soft blanket of silence. Perhaps I should forget about time and write a haiku about snow instead, or perhaps one about silence. The problem of being a haiku poet is that I see them all around me.

Wrapped up in my heavy kimono, I continue to gaze out of the window as I wait for the water to boil. The boats down in the harbour are like a haikai zen painting with their blanket of snow. I never tire of this view; it was what made me decide to rent this old house in the first place. For a haiku poet, it is like a constant stream of inspiration as the seasons flow by my window and I look down at the boats, shimmering in the summer sun or bathing in the blue of winter nights.

The sound of the water boiling pulls me away from my reflections and I set about making my tea, then take it back to the warmth of my tatami and turn my mind to plan today's lesson for one of my more advanced haiku students. He has an impressive degree of talent for a seventeen year old, but unfortunately this is smothered by his obvious ambition and impatience to become a successful haiku teacher, hence the private haiku tuition paid for by his equally ambitious parents. While I welcome the income to pay the rent, I find it hard work to inspire within him a love for the essence of haiku rather than the academic history and development of the art, which is where he sees his future career as a teacher.

On our very first lesson, when I asked him why he wanted to become a haiku poet, he quite frankly told me that he saw great potential in its growing popularity outside of Japan. I could not suppress my smile at his frankness but found his intentions rather mercenary. I remember pointing out, as politely as I could, that his ambition needed to have its roots in a love of haiku. Sadly, that is where I am still, trying to let haiku touch his heart rather than his head, trying in my own humble way to emulate the haiku master Shiki who instructed his students to still the mind and let the heart speak of the haiku.

By the time I have finished my tea, I have devised my teaching plan for the day. He will not like it, but I must continue to try to cultivate a love for this most Japanese of all Japanese art forms. The same gift which was given to me by my own haiku teacher Ryokan, a Zen monk to whom I owe a debt I can never repay. It was he who found me collapsed and close to death by the door of his monastery and it is due to his care, compassion and wisdom that I was able to rebuild my life as a haiku poet.

Getting up, I start my day as ever by sitting in zazen meditation, looking out at the small garden which I have created over the thirty years or so that I have lived here. The garden looks delightful with the fall of snow upon the red wooden bridge spanning the little winding stream. I find my mind slipping easily into that internal Zen space, which I have also developed since being found by the Zen monk.

I remember being awakened that first morning by the low tones of the great monastery bell calling the monks to prayer. I had no idea where I was or I had got there but felt far too weak to even try to find out and slipped back into a deep sleep. When I awoke again it was daylight, and sitting in perfect silence and stillness beside me was the robed figure of a Zen monk.

I remember feeling quite intimidated by the monk, whose broad face and fierce looking eyebrows made him look more like a samurai than a monk. He must have seen my fear, for he very gently put his hand on my shoulder and smiled.

'Have no fear,' he said. 'My name is Ryokan. And you are perfectly safe here.'

'Where am I?' I managed to whisper in a very dry voice.

'You are in a Zen monastery,' the monk replied. 'You were found by our temple door. So, we have taken you in and given you refuge.'

'How long have I been here?'

'You have been asleep for almost two days,' he replied. 'Where do you belong?'

A simple question, but one which I found impossible to answer, as I realised that I had no memory of anything.

'Have no fear,' the monk said again, reading the distress in my face. 'You must rest now. Be patient, it will all come back to you.'

Despite the gentle monk's reassurance, however, it never did come back. I still have no memory of the events leading up to his finding me at the temple door.

Despite his fierce appearance, Ryokan proved to be one of the most gentle and thoughtful souls I have ever known. He later told me that his duty within the monastery was that of novice master, guiding the young monks through their novitiate year.

When I eventually regained enough strength to stand and walk, Ryokan showed me around the monastery, introducing me to some of the basic principles of the Zen way of life. Perhaps he felt rather responsible toward me, as it was he who found me. Whatever the reason, this gentle monk took me under his wing like one of his novices and helped to rebuild my life.

The first thing that struck me was how immaculately clean everything was. I remember Ryokan smiling when I said this, and he went on to explain that the monks cleaned and polished the whole monastery from top to toe every day as a form of Zen meditation and part of their simple way of life of work and prayer.

'Simplicity is an essential element of Zen,' he said. 'Creating a clear and simple interior space within the mind is reflected in the exterior space in which one lives, free of clutter and distraction. As one develops in Zen, one grows to love simplicity and space in all things.'

In keeping with Ryokan's teaching, I found the monastery almost totally devoid of anything that was not essential, each room consisting of nothing more than a polished floor and the space for Zen to be practiced. I remember seeing monks working away at various tasks, cleaning, cooking and gardening, but all in perfect silence and in a calm and unhurried way.

'They are still practicing Zen,' Ryokan explained, as he saw me watching the monks intently. 'Zen is a way of life, and an attitude of mind. The monks cultivate this attitude by sitting in classical zazen meditation, but then continue in this Zen state of mind throughout the day in their daily work. Everything is done in the Zen state of meditating on the present moment.'

'I am afraid I have no choice but to think of the here and now,' I said. 'For I can still remember nothing. Not even my name.'

'You must be patient with yourself,' the monk said. 'It is obvious that you have been through some kind of traumatic experience. Memory loss is quite common in such circumstances. You need to rest and let your mind and your body heal. Of course, you are free to stay with us until you feel well enough to leave.'

All that happened over thirty years ago, and Ryokan and I have become close friends over the years. While in time my body healed, my mind has never recovered from whatever traumatic event happened all that time ago.

As I finish my morning zazen meditation, I set about preparing breakfast. A bowl of rice and some lemon tea, the lemon is a little extravagance which I picked up some time ago. I never set out to be an aesthetic, but Ryokan my Zen teacher warned me that while Zen does not insist upon living an austere way of life, it somehow just happens.

'Zen and simplicity are inseparable,' he said, 'and both lead to a clarity of thought and vision. In the words of the Zen master Dogon, Zen creates a clear eye, free of the dust of distractions that obscure the true vision of reality.'

Over the years this Zen simplicity of vision gently invaded all my senses and tastes, and I now understand how some Zen hermits eventually prefer to live on little more than tea and rice. I am not at that stage, but I do find my lemon tea a refreshing way to start my day.

After breakfast I set to cleaning the house, yet another influence of my time in the monastery, cleaning and polishing everything. It never takes too long, as my house is very small and of course free of clutter. As always, I finish by polishing the small oak tebaru on which I write my haiku, with the finest beeswax polish. Bringing out the best in the wood somehow prepares my mind to bring out the best in my haiku.

With the house ready for my student, I go over my lesson plan once again, with simplicity being the essential element. Haiku of all things should be kept free and clear of too much clutter, which only blocks spontaneity and inspiration, hence the traditional observance of using only seventeen onji spaced out into three lines. Some very traditional haiku masters still insist on the oral reading of a haiku being done in one single breath, to preserve simplicity. Personally, I feel that this detracts from the beauty and mystery of the haiku, and that the pauses between the lines are almost as essential as the words.

I clearly remember my own first haiku lesson from Ryokan, in which he simply lay a few haiku out and asked me to pick up the first one that appealed to me. He advised me not to think too much about it, but just go with my heart. I chose one by a poet named Meitsetsu:

Traveling priest
vanishing in the mist
trailed by his bell.

'And now tell me why you chose it,' Ryokan said. 'And once again, don't think about it too much.'

'Because my identity has also vanished in the mist,' I replied.

'Good,' he said. 'Anything else?'

'The bell,' I replied. 'I remember hearing the bell. I was walking through trees, in the dark, and I heard the bell. It was the bell that led me to your temple door.'

'Interesting,' Ryokan said. 'You see how haiku can open the mind. And now I want you to go away and create your own haiku and show it to me.'

'I would not know where to begin,' I said.

'Three lines,' Ryokan replied. 'Five onji in the first, seven in the second, and five in the third line. Written from the heart, for that is the secret door to unlocking your inner mind.'

And so, with this first lesson in haiku, I set out to write my own. But where to begin? I sat in my room in the monastery staring at my blank sheet of paper, as empty as my memory. I finally admitted defeat and went for a walk in the grounds, with the moon casting its shadows among the trees. And then I heard the monastery bell, calling the monks to prayer and in that moment, I became a haiku poet.

When I met Ryokan the next day, I rather tentatively laid my haiku on the table:

> Moonlight in the trees
> echoing through the shadows
> the toll of a bell.

'Interesting,' he said again. 'It is your story of how you were led here. But there is a fragrance of mystery about it. I also like the way you describe the sound of the bell as echoing through shadows, as though the sound is feeling its way through the trees. Perhaps feeling its way to where you came from.'

Ryokan then searched through one of his haiku books until he found what he was looking for.

'What do you make of this?' he asked. 'It is a haiku written by a poet called Uko.'

> The nightingale sings
> in the echo of the bell
> tolled at evening.

'Similar to mine,' I said, handing the book back to him.

'Very similar,' Ryokan agreed. 'The difference being that Uko wrote that hundreds of years ago after a lifetime of writing haiku. You have written this after your first lesson. It is clear to me that haiku is the path which we must take to unlock the mystery of who you are. And looking at this haiku, I think that we may find that this is not the first one that you have written.'

Under Ryokan's instruction, my haiku deepened over the years and I actually started to get some published. Eventually I became a haiku teacher and was able to rent this little house overlooking the harbour. Haiku became my ikigai, my way of life and reason for living, but sadly it never did open the door of my mind to reveal who I was before the bell led me to the door of the Zen monastery on that moonlit night.

2

In winter moonlight
silver from the spider's web
frozen in the air.
Shijin

Ryokan became my mentor, not only in haiku but in the art of Zen, from which haiku originally grew as a means of teaching novice monks how to meditate upon the reality that exists beneath the surface of all material things.

'In Zen, the monk must first know himself, then learn to be himself, and then finally learn to forget himself, to live in the reality of the here and now', Ryokan said.

The monk went on to explain that in zazen meditation, the aim is to rediscover our experience of life afresh, with a clear eye.

'We do this by silencing the mind from its endless stream of distracting thoughts, which create a false impression', he said. 'To free the mind from illusions which detract from the spontaneous joy of living here and now in the present moment. The past is gone, the future has not yet happened, the reality is now.'

I remember being quite excited at the prospect of being taught how to meditate by a Zen monk, but confessed that I did not see how his simple instruction of silencing the mind was possible. 'How can I stop thinking?' I asked.

As always, my question was answered with a patient smile. 'By learning how to listen to silence', he said.

Ryokan went on to explain that to achieve this, one must first find a silent space to be still, then in that stillness begin to listen to one's breath. This slows the mind down to think only of the here and now. After that, one must start to listen only to the silence between the breaths, until eventually the mind forgets about the breaths and thinks only of the silence. Then it is only a matter of following that silent path into the Zen space that exists beneath the mind.

'The silence that Zen seeks to find is not simply an absence of sound,' Ryokan said. 'It is a place of silence, a feeling of silence, a silent attitude of mind.'

I did not realise it then, but that Zen place which the monk helped me to find was to become as much a home to me as this little house on the hill. And from that Zen place, my haiku flourished and created a new life for me.

I adopted Ryokan's inspirational style of teaching, aimed at developing my student's insights and cultivating perceptiveness rather than focusing on the precise form and established norms of haiku. The aim was to open the mind beyond the rather strict traditions some haiku masters still adhere to, insisting upon each haiku having a season word and a cutting word after the second line and so on.

'Haiku is the most Japanese of art forms,' Ryokan said. 'And its austere simplicity is part of its beauty and reflects its roots within Zen. But it is exactly this simplicity of form that makes haiku universal and open to all cultures. Its purity and simplicity is like rain, with every drop a pool of reflection of wherever it falls. The aim is always the same, to capture the essence of the natural beauty in which we are immersed. To express the human need to record beauty and to invite others to delight in what we see.'

As I take my mid-morning tea, I leaf through my collection of haikai art until I find a suitable piece, 'Descending Geese in Autumn' by Kubo. I can only hope that it can convince my young student to see the world of haiku beyond its rigid scholastic forms. He will no doubt become a successful haiku teacher, as his knowledge and skill are as obvious as his ambition. But to become a master, one must take all the traditions of the past and synthesise them to expand the art form, not constrict it within rigid rules of structure and form.

With the extra money I started to make from teaching haiku, I was eventually able to move out from a basic rented room and rent this little house with its perfect view of the fishing harbour. When I first moved in, the garden was badly overgrown and neglected, but I could see its potential, particularly in the little mud-covered stream that ran through it. Over the years I have managed to slowly transform the garden, and it is now a little haven of tranquility.

At the back of the garden there is a small red brick wall, very weathered by the wind and rain, but in my eyes that makes it all the more perfect. When I first took the keys of the house, I sat by the window looking down the hill at the fishing harbour at sunset, feeling very much at home. Then as the sun set, I took my customary walk in the moonlight, looking for inspiration in the garden. It was then that I saw the spider's web hanging between the red bricks and glistening with frost in the moonlight. The spider had long gone, and the web looked quite old and very fragile, but it was perfect for my first haiku in my new home:

> In winter moonlight
> silver from the spider's web
> frozen in the air.

That night, a storm blew up, with heavy rain and high winds. When I went out into the garden in the morning, the web had gone. But I had captured the haiku of its transient beauty before it was lost. Haiku seeks not only to capture beauty but to suggest its fragile impermanence. The form of haiku does not allow the poet to use metaphor explicitly, but rather to suggest a fragrance of the emotion one aims to convey. From the web of a spider, for example, the poet may try to express the vulnerability of all life upon this fragile planet.

With my preparations complete, I finish my tea and await the arrival of my student, who knocks upon my door precisely on time, his way of demonstrating the proper level of respect.

'Ohayo gozaimasu, haiku master,' he says, bowing very formally. He is seventeen years old, but dresses and behaves like he is forty. I wonder who the real seventeen-year-old Toshiro is and not this mini replica of his idea of a classical haiku poet.

'Ohayo gozaimasu, Toshiro-san,' I reply, returning his bow. 'Please do come in and be seated.'

'And how is your haiku coming on?' I ask as we take our seats beside my freshly polished tebaru.

'I have completed something which I hope reflects the homework you gave me,' he replies, laying an immaculate piece of rice paper on the tebaru with a great show of humility, which fails to hide his obvious pride in his efforts.

'Do tell me something about it before I read it,' I say. 'The inspiration for the haiku is of course just as important as the poem.'

He obviously disagrees, but politely explains how he saw three monks walking in a straight line, and how this reminded him of the three lines of haiku.

'Interesting,' I say, borrowing one of my Zen mentor's stock responses. 'Do tell me more.'

'When we last met, haiku master, you suggested that I explore Shiki's insistence that each line of the haiku must convey a fragrance of the other two lines.'

'And your haiku achieves this?'

'Perhaps if I might be allowed to read it to you, haiku master,' he replies, finding it hard to hide his impatience.

'Very well,' I say, smiling. 'Let us see what you have written.'

Toshiro lifts his haiku up from the tebaru with studied formality. Sitting up very straight, he holds it at arm's length to maximise the gravity of the moment, before proceeding:

> Three Zen monks walking
> following a narrow path
> making one shadow.

'This is good, Toshiro-san,' I say, honestly quite impressed. He is making progress and there is depth to this. 'And what do you see as the fragrance that unites each line?'

'The fragrance is in their journeying together,' he replies.

'Yes, I do see that. But do you think that there may be a deeper fragrance of the essence of Zen within each line? The first line introducing the Zen monks, the second suggesting that they all closely follow the narrow path of Zen, and the third line suggesting that the one shadow they make together is the shadow of the mystery of Zen, which they explore together to attain enlightenment.'

'Thank you, haiku master,' Toshiro says, placing the haiku back on the tebaru. 'Your interpretation does take the haiku further than I realised.'

'Tell me, Toshiro-san,' I say, picking up the haiku to read over it. 'Why do you think Shiki used the term 'fragrance', and not for example simply use the word 'reflection' or 'echo', to describe the common theme running through the three lines?'

'Shiki was known for his poetic use of words,' he replies.

'True, but he was also famous for what he left unsaid, to invite the reader of his haiku to take a step beyond the words. In other words, to go beyond the form of the haiku, to go from the known into the unknown, the part of the haiku that hints at the mystery that lies beneath the form.'

My student's silence speaks volumes. We have crossed swords over this question before. He, like many haiku scholars, views the form and ritual use of traditional Japanese expressions and symbolism as the essence of haiku's beauty. Whereas I, like many other poets including the great Shiki, see the form as integral to the haiku's beauty but secondary to its essence, that greater depth of beauty that transcends words.

'With great respect, haiku master,' Toshiro says, 'Master Shiki also insisted that the shasei, the objective representation of what inspired the haiku, is always superior to anything that the poet could subjectively draw from their imagination.'

'I am impressed, Toshiro-san,' I say honestly. 'And I congratulate you on a fine haiku and an equally fine defense of the traditionalist school of thought. However, Shiki also believed that the form of haiku should not be allowed to inhibit its essence. As you know, haiku originated as a form of Zen meditation, to focus upon the essence of the experience and to capture that essence in the simplest and most direct way, for others to enter into the experience.'

'Precisely my point, haiku master,' Toshiro says. 'So the shasai, the experience, must be kept simple and free from metaphor. And it was the haiku master Buson who taught his students to learn about the bamboo from the bamboo. In other words, keep it focused on the experience.'

'Very impressive, Toshiro,' I concede. 'But in doing so, the shasai must also contain a fragrance of the underlying makato, the deeper essence of the subject. For example, the lemon with which I make my tea. My haiku about this would of course describe the lemon in the most pure and simple way possible, but also contain the fragrance of the zest of the lemon, which is its essence. So whenever one reads the haiku, they may even smell the fragrance and remember its freshness and sharpness of taste. Do you follow?'

Toshiro does not reply, but simply bows thoughtfully. Perhaps I am beginning to make slow progress at last.

'Shiki also suggested that haiku could be more free, and draw upon other elements and forms of art. Which brings me to my subject for today's lesson. What do you think of this haikai?' I say, placing Kubo's 'Descending Geese in Autumn' on the tebaru.

The look of indifference on my young student's face reveals quite clearly that he does not think very much of it.

'I suggest that here the artist is using ink as poets would use our words to express the subtle beauty of the moment. Don't you agree?'

'So sorry, haiku master,' Toshiro says, 'but they don't even look like geese. And they are even difficult to distinguish from the clouds in the background. They are obviously not real, but exist only in the mind of the artist. This is exactly what Buson warned against.'

'But does it not invite us to look beyond the geese and into the clouds?' I reply. 'Remember Shiki's use of the word fragrance: a fragrance lingers in the air like the essence of the subject, inviting the reader to enter deeper into the haiku with each consecutive line. To use the art to lead us beyond the obvious. Any painter can paint geese, Toshiro-san, but it takes a master to paint them in the form of clouds.'

'And how does this apply to haiku?' Toshiro asks, still struggling to make the connection.

'Haiku is the essence of Japan,' I reply. 'The most Japanese of all art forms. And we must express that essence in all its fragrance. It is the essence that is important, not the form. It is not just the form of the geese that delights us, Toshiro-san, it is the fragrance, the essence of what they represent. Words, even the beautiful words of haiku, can only invite the mind to go beyond the words to explore the essence.'

When I finally bring our lesson to a close, I invite my student to write a haiku about haiku to bring to our next session. He bows respectfully, but I can see that he is struggling with the idea.

'The aim is to explore the haiku itself, rather than the subject,' I explain. 'For example, during my morning meditation of my garden, I noticed a few dead leaves still clinging to the tree. This made me think of leaves being like the fragile three lines of haiku. But then my eyes were drawn to a single green bud on one the branches, like a promise of spring amidst the snow. And this made me think of new and fresh haiku being born in the spring. The old leaves and the new green bud are from the same tree that it is constantly changing, like haiku.'

Toshiro bows very formally and thanks me for a most interesting lesson, but I know that he remains unconvinced. Perhaps I have gone a little too far in trying to free his mind from rigidly following tradition. He may even decide to find a more traditional haiku teacher who is of a similar mind set about form and essence. Or perhaps I have sown a seed that may one day take root if he experiences a fragrance of the mystery that lies at the heart of haiku. It may even expand his mind to make that transcendent leap into that inner reality which haiku can only hint at.

What I would really love to see is this talented seventeen-year-old boy knocking on my door again with his hair blowing freely in the breeze and wearing a casual multi-coloured shirt, his eyes full of the love of the essence of haiku. Haiku should, after all, free the poet to experience the beauty of life and not constrict them to imitate the experiences of others.

3

Sitting at anchor
fishing boats in calm water
quiet reflections.
Shijin

When Toshiro has gone, I step out into my Zen garden to rest my mind in that tranquil space. I find teaching haiku both rewarding and exhausting at the same time. Without the skill and patience of my own haiku teacher Ryokan, however, I would never have become a haiku teacher. And so, I owe a debt that needs to be repaid by passing on my insights to inspire future haiku poets.

Sometimes, however, a student comes along who actually inspires me, and that is always very refreshing. Ame, for example, a wandering beggar dressed in rags, who showed up at my door asking how to become a haiku master. He had no formal teaching, but had a soul that was clearly overflowing with the love of haiku.

He needed almost no instruction from me. I believe that even the haiku master Shiki himself would have delighted in Ame. I passed on Shiki's classic advice to him, to simply write from his own experience in a clear and simple way, to detach the mind and enter into the essence of the haiku moment.

As I walk slowly through my garden, following the winding pebble path which mirrors the flow of the stream, I think back to when Ame and I walked here together that morning when he called at my house. His haiku were already delightful in their fresh simplicity. When he took his leave, he told me of his plans to live a simple life in an old boathouse and dedicate his life to haiku. As a parting gift, I created a haiku about our time in the garden. Two poets, like two leaves flowing in a stream of time.

That was actually the second time that our paths had met – the first was a few years earlier, when I came across him sitting in zazen writing haiku about pebbles on a beach. Even then I could detect a natural talent in that simple little haiku. When we met the second time at my house, that talent had blossomed through living the life of a wandering poet, almost like the great haiku master Basho in his itinerant travels all through Japan. I was struck in particular with Ame's haiku of Mt. Fujiyama, and felt that it was as good as anything I had read of the holy mountain.

Occasionally I will take a student out here to walk with me in the Zen garden to follow the pebble path, and then the memory of the young itinerant haiku poet and his pebble haiku always comes to mind. He was that kind of person, once seen never forgotten.

I ask my students to think only of the pebbles under our feet and to choose one that attracts their attention. Invariably, they all find one particular pebble from the great variety of colours, textures and shapes which resonates with something inside them. Then as we sit by the stream flowing under the bridge, I ask them to reflect upon why they chose their pebble and to write a haiku about it.

I find it interesting that very few of my students ever choose a pebble for its obvious beauty, but one that is imperfect in some way, finding something in it that resonated within themselves. For me, the lesson within the pebbles is that we all have imperfections which are part of our unique personalities.

Today, as I walk the Zen pebble path, my mind turns to the millions of years that have passed in the making of each pebble under my feet. Each one with its own unique characteristics created by exposure to time and the elements, ground down by the waves, bleached by the sun and the sea, to reveal that own unique beauty and with their own unique story locked within them, until some wandering haiku poet like Ame sits down beside them and writes about the mystery.

In Zen moments such as this, a single pebble can lead into an inward journey into that Zen space, where one is reminded of the universal unity within all things. When one returns from that Zen space, the beauty of the natural world within which we are immersed is re-experienced and we see it afresh with enlightened eyes, clear of the dust of distraction. Zen is not an escape from reality but an entering into it at an ever-deeper level of realization.

The winter sunlight glistening on the snow now convinces me that this is not a day to spend indoors writing haiku, but to get out and live some haiku moments. And so, getting well wrapped up, I head off down the hill to have lunch by the harbour, stopping at the little shop to buy some of Madam Yoko's freshly made fish cakes and noodle soup.

I smile as I think of what my student Toshiro's response might be if I dared to suggest that Madam Yoko was almost poetic in creating these deliciously simple things, which encapsulate the fragrance of this little fishing village in which I have made my home.

Ever since my mentor Ryokan introduced me to haiku, the sea has been a fathomless source of inspiration. It is constantly changing to reflect the light and the moods of the weather. In winter sunlight, such as today, it is a shimmering mirror of light that delights the soul. In moonlight nights, it is a fathomless source of mystery.

Ryokan's promise, that haiku would be the gate that would eventually open the mystery of my identity, was never fulfilled. Even after all these years, I am still known simply as Shijin, a poet. I even owe my name to Ryokan, who insisted that my haiku must have a signature.

'You would not be the first haiku poet to choose a name for yourself,' he said. 'The haiku master Issa, for example, chose his name meaning one cup of tea, after his love of the tea ceremony. And the great master Shiki chose his name meaning cuckoo, simply because he loved the sound the bird made. So then, my friend, by what name will your haiku be known?'

The thought of being called after a bird, or worse still, a cup of tea, held no appeal. Therefore, I decided simply upon Shijin, poet, much to Ryokan's delight.

'The first haiku poet to be named so,' he laughed. 'Shijin it shall be, at least until haiku reveals who you really are.'

Of course, it never did. And so, to the good people of this fishing village, and to Madam Yoko, I remain simply Shijin the poet. Her restaurant is a modest little place right on the harbour, but her simple seafood is truly delightful. She now hands me the little box of her delicious fishcakes and the bowl of noodle soup. I bid her good day, then go in search of a suitable spot for an old poet to have his lunch.

The harbour is almost empty of boats, as it is still just past midday and the fishermen will not return until nearly sunset, but I pass the time of day with a few other old people as I stroll around enjoying the winter sunshine. Finding a little sun trap by some fish crates, I indulge myself with a taste of one of the fish cakes, which prove as delicious as ever, particularly when eaten out in the fresh air. The noodle soup proves delicious also, and still piping hot as I sip it from the bowl and let my mind wander back to my first visit here.

As the months passed by in the monastery with no sign of my memory returning, Ryokan very gently suggested that perhaps it was time for me to leave.

'This is a very secluded place here, Shijin-san,' he said. 'And perhaps you now need to mix with people in the outside world a little more to hopefully stir up some memories.'

Unable to hide my disappointment, I confessed to him that I had started to hope that I may actually be allowed to stay in the monastery and progress in the Zen way of life.

'This life is not for everyone, Shijin-san,' he said. 'Quite often I have to guide some of my novices to leave the monastery and find another way of life more suited to their personality.'

Then he smiled and began to tell me one of his Zen stories, about three novices who were asked to draw a haikai picture of what they saw as the perfect monastery. The first drew a great oak door, to represent how one entered the monastery to leave the outside world behind. The second drew a monastery overlooking the sea, to represent how the monks could spend their life in quiet contemplation of the beauty of the world. But when the third novice showed his haikai to his novice master, it simply showed a mountain with its summit hidden in the clouds, to represent how the perfect monastery is hidden in the mind of each individual.

'You have made good progress in the way of Zen here, Shijin-san,' Ryokan continued, 'but Zen is a state of mind and not confined to these walls. You must learn to find your unique Zen place where you can continue in the way of enlightenment.'

Ryokan went on to tell me that he had already made arrangements for me to take lodgings in the fishing village just along the coast.

'Madam Yoko, who runs the harbour restaurant, is happy to let you have her spare room at a very reasonable rent.'

'But I have no money,' I replied. 'And I could not impose upon your generosity any longer.'

'No need to worry, Shijin-san,' he said. 'I have also arranged for you to work on the fishing boat of an old friend of mine, who is finding the work too much for him to do alone. He will pay you a fair wage, enough anyway to pay Madam Yoko for your room and board.'

The next morning, Ryokan and I set off for the fishing village to meet the people whom I would now be living and working with. He took me first to the harbour restaurant, frequented by the local fishermen.

'Madam Yoko, this is Shijin,' Ryokan said, by way of introduction to the little friendly faced woman who had just emerged from her kitchen, wiping flour from her hands on her apron.

'So, this is my new lodger, eh?' she said, eyeing me up. 'He's a bit skinny, isn't he? He will need feeding up if he is to work on Natsuki's boat.'

'You are as well informed as ever, I see,' Ryokan said, smiling.

'O-hayo gosaimasu, Yoko okusama,' I said, bowing politely.

'Okusama, eh? He is a polite one, Ryokan-san,' my new landlady said, giving me a little bow in return. 'O-hayo gosaimasu, Shijin-san. I'm sure that you and I will get on nicely. Come through and let me show you to your room.'

The room proved to be very basic but perfectly clean, just leading off from Madam Yoko's kitchen and already filled with the delicious aroma of whatever she was making for lunch. I dropped off my few things then Ryokan and I set out to find the old fisherman I was going to work for.

We found Natsuki by his boat, mending nets that looked as old and tired as he did.

'O-hayo gosaimasu, Natsuki-san,' Ryokan said, as the old fisherman looked me up and down. 'This is Shinjin-san.'

'Done any fishing before?' he asked, ignoring the need for introductions.

'I'm afraid I don't know,' I replied.

'Shinjin-san has lost his memory,' Ryokan said. 'Remember, we talked about it?'

Natsuki gave me another long appraising look. 'Tomorrow morning then,' he said. 'Sailing at six. Don't be late.'

'Domo origato, Natsuki-san, I said, with mixed feelings about being accepted by my new employer.

'I think he likes you,' Ryokan said, as we walked back to the harbour restaurant for lunch.

'He has a strange way of showing it,' I replied.

'His pride is hurt. He has been fiercely independent all these years, but is now getting too old to manage on his own. It can't be easy, Shinjin-san.'

In contrast to old Natsuki, Madam Yoko made us very welcome once again and sat us down to a delicious lunch, which she refused to accept payment for.

'It's all included in your rent,' she said. 'And how could I ask for payment from a holy monk?'

Ryokan thanked her for her kindness, then left me to get settled in, promising to drop by in a few days to see how I was getting on. I spent the rest of the day wandering around the fishing village. Then, after another fine meal in the evening, I asked Madam Yoko for an early call and went to bed. I let my eyes rest on the view from the single little window as the moon came up over the harbour, until I finally fell asleep.

The next morning, I set off early with Madam Yoko's hot steaming bowl of oatmeal and tea setting me up for the day. In addition, she had packed a little lunchbox before seeing me off at the door with a maternal warning to be careful.

I had hoped to arrive before Natsuki, to create a good impression, but found him already at work and preparing to get under way.

'Climb aboard,' he said, by way of greeting. 'And cast off that rope.'

And with that, he bid me sit in the bow of the boat and took her out to sea. It was still dark when he dropped the sail at the fishing grounds, with a calm sea around us.

'Let's get the nets down,' Natsuki said, showing me what to do with as few words as I had come to expect from him.

'Not bad,' he said, when we had finished and sat in the boat letting the nets drift with the tide. 'I think you might have done this before.'

This took me very much by surprise. 'What makes you say that?' I asked.

'The way you got into the boat and cast off the rope,' he replied. 'And you seem to have good sea legs and can turn your hand easy enough to the nets.'

This was praise indeed from the old fisherman, and I detected a distinct warming in his manner toward me. With this to ponder upon, we spent a pleasant day at sea and returned in the evening with a decent catch of fish.

'Not bad at all, Shinjin-san,' Natsuki said as we dropped off the crates of fish at the merchant. 'See you tomorrow.'

Feeling very pleased with the fact that I seemed to have got the job, I returned to the tender care of my landlady Madam Yoko. And so, my life settled into this new routine, fishing by day and quiet evenings with my view of the harbour.

I continued with writing haiku about the sea and being out in the boat. The ever-inquisitive Madam Yoko came across them one day when she was cleaning my room and lost no time in making sure that the whole village knew about the fine haiku poet she had for a lodger. She then talked me into giving little recitals of my haiku to her evening guests. Fortune smiled upon me once again when, at her prompting, I entered a haiku competition and won first prize of five hundred yen and a commission to write a book of haiku. With this, my reputation as a haiku poet grew locally and I began to get requests to teach it, mostly to the children of rich merchants. What had begun as a form of Zen meditation had somehow developed into a well-paid way of life. The irony of this amused my friend Ryokan immensely.

'The path of Zen takes many unseen twists and turns,' he said.

In time, I was earning enough from my haiku to leave Madam Yoko's guesthouse and rent my own little place at the top of the hill, but we have remained good friends ever since and I never fail to call in for lunch on my trips around the harbour.

I continued to help old Natsuki until eventually he became much too old to continue fishing and finally had to sell his boat to make ends meet and keep a roof above his head. It was a very sad day when I stood by his side and watched the new owner sail Natsuki's boat away. I had grown very close to this fine old man during our long trips at sea and could feel his pain as his boat sailed over the horizon. Whenever I visited him after that, I would always find him sitting by his window gazing out to sea. You can take the old man out of the sea, but you can't take the sea out of the old man.

Perhaps old Natsuki had been right on that very first day when he said that I might have been a fisherman in my past, as I did seem to take to the work very easily and grew to love my time on the water. Ryokan's plan for my memory to return through living and working with these fine people, however, did not bear fruit. Over the years I have just had to accept that whoever I was will remain lost to me forever.

With the harbour gulls now swooping around me for morsels of my fishcakes, I take pity upon them and scatter the crumbs on the harbour wall. Then, with a last look around, I return Madam Yoko's bowl and head off back up the hill for home.

4

The steps of the monk
leave no footprints in the snow
on the path of Zen.
Shijin

As usual, I'm breathing a bit heavily when I make my way back up the hill and looking forward to sitting down with a bowl of tea, but I am stopped in my tracks as I see a stranger hanging around my door. I get very few visitors, and even then, I usually know when to expect them. There is something about this man's bearing that tells me that this is no social call.

'Can I help you?' I ask, as the man turns to watch me walking up my path.

He is polite enough and bids me good day, then says that he is looking for the poet Shijin who lives here.

'I am Shijin,' I reply. 'How can I help you?' I ask again, with a growing sense of disquiet.

'My name is Inspector Kaneko,' he replies. 'I am making certain inquiries into the identity of a man who has been found dead a little further along the coast from here.'

'You had better come inside, Inspector,' I say, quite taken off guard by this revelation.

'And how does this affect me?' I ask once we are both sat down.

'The man was found this morning in an isolated hut by some walkers,' he continued. 'There was no sign of any foul play, but he had nothing to identify him. Except this, a haiku which was found on his person. It appears to have been signed by you, sir. Do you happen to recognise it?'

The policeman placed the haiku like a piece of evidence in one of those plastic envelopes on my tebaru, with his very alert eyes searching mine. I felt my blood run cold, not through any fear of him, but from my recognition of the haiku.

Watching drifting leaves
haiku poets by a stream
quiet reflections.
Shijin

'Yes, Inspector,' I reply finally, trying to keep my voice steady. 'That is one of my haiku.'

'And have you any idea who you might have given it to?'

'Yes, I gave it to a young poet only the other day when he came to me for instruction.'

'Can you describe him?'

'Young, dark hair, very thin, and quite unkempt looking, from living rough for quite some time,' I said, seeing Ame standing right where the Inspector was only a few days ago.

'In that case, I am afraid that your description appears to fit the person who was found dead, sir. May I ask you what his name was?'

'His name is Ame.'

'I am sorry, sir,' the policeman said. 'I realise that this has come as a shock. But I am afraid that I have to ask if you would agree to accompany me to identify him.'

From being a normal, pleasant day, this had now turned into some dreadful nightmare. Still quite shocked, I got up and followed the policeman out and into his waiting car.

'It won't take long, sir,' the Inspector said. 'An hour or so along the coast.' As if that made things any easier. But I suppose he was only trying to be kind.

As we drove past the harbour, I looked out the window at the spot where I had been sitting eating fish cakes only a short while ago. And now I was going to identify the dead body of a homeless young man who had been discussing haiku with me only a few days ago, asking me how to become a haiku master.

'Are you alright, sir?' asks the policeman.

'I'm fine, Inspector,' I lie, for I am devastated. My life revolves around writing about transiently beautiful mysterious things, but there is nothing transiently beautiful about a homeless man being found dead in an old hut. As we drive on in silence along the coast road, I think about Ame walking along here after leaving my house that day. His journey all around Japan drawing to its close, his heart set upon seeing his old boathouse once again. But he never got there, dying alone before he could make it home.

'It's just up there, sir, beyond those trees,' the Inspector says as he pulls the police car over and stops.

As we start to walk up through the trees, I begin to experience a growing sense of disquiet, and for some strange reason, Uko's haiku about the bell tolling at evening strangely comes to mind. I realise that it is in this walking through trees in strange circumstances that reminds me of that night when I wandered through the trees following the bell to the monastery door. Walking through trees again is somehow taking me back too close to whatever traumatic event my mind has blocked out from my past.

As we continue through the woods, my mind goes back to Ryokan's initial guidance in trying to help me remember who I am and where I came from, by using his skill in zazen meditation to try and unlock my memory.

'Zen cannot be taught intellectually, but must be learned intuitively,' he explained. 'We must all find our own way to that Zen place within us. The Zen master can only give guidance, like a finger pointing to the moon, showing the path the student must take. And the first step along that path is always to sit in zazen to listen in stillness to what we intuitively feel is the right way for us.'

When I confessed that I found it difficult to understand how I could intuitively know about something which I could not understand intellectually, Ryokan responded with his customary patient smile.

'How do the snow geese find their way home in due season?' he said. 'Or the salmon return to the place where they were born after many years at sea? By intuition, they feel their way home. And so, you must learn to listen to what you intuitively know. The Zen master Dogon explained that in sitting quietly in zazen, the grass around you grows all by itself. In other words, you learn about Zen by sitting in Zen. It must be experienced firsthand through silence, for it is beyond words. If you were suddenly able to see a new colour, how could you describe it in words to someone who could not see it? You could only advise them how to try and see it for themselves. The Zen master can only be a finger pointing to the moon for you to experience it for yourself.'

And so, I began my internal journey by sitting in zazen and feeling my way forward, like a blind man trusting his instincts to find his way. I can only describe the feeling which I experienced in that first zazen session as like being in a boat at sea, feeling the sea flowing beneath the boat and then slowly the boat becoming more still as the sea grew quiet all around me. Then the boat the sea and I became as one in a stillness and silence that I had never experienced before.

I discussed my experiences with Ryokan, who seemed pleased with my progress and my analogy of being at sea.

'The path of Zen takes many forms,' he said. 'And leads us in many ways. With you it led to the sea, with others perhaps to the mountains or the forest, or even the sky. That is why the Zen masters all insist that the path of the enlightened ones leaves no track for others to follow. We must all find our own way.'

When Ryokan felt that I had made enough progress, he said that we should now continue to use my intuitive senses to lead me back to where I came from.

'To discover who you are, Shinjin-san, we must discover where you came from,' he said. 'Remember the salmon, let your intuition guide you like the salmon, feeling its way back through the flow of the water to the place where it was born.'

In my next zazen session, I let my mind go back to that night when I found my way to the monastery by following the sound of the bell. But then, as I attempted to retrace my steps in my mind back through the woods to where I had come from, all the calm serenity that I had come to associate with zazen was suddenly replaced by a feeling of uneasiness, which increased with every mental step which I took back into those trees.

When I described my experience to Ryokan, he told me that this actually confirmed his suspicions that my amnesia was the result of my mind being unable to cope with some traumatic experience in my past. When I tried to retrace my steps back there, those traumatic feelings began to resurface.

'Now we have to very sensitively explore what happened to you, Shinjin-san,' he said. 'So, we must continue with your zazen meditation and see where it leads you. Zen is a doorway within the physical world that leads to the eternal now. In that Zen place your past and your present must become one, to free your mind from whatever it cannot face in the past. So now you must walk in Zen.'

Ryokan went on to explain that in physically walking back the way I had come to the monastery that night, my mind and my body may begin to relive that night.

So that night, with Ryokan at my side, I slowly began to walk into the woods. Almost immediately I felt my pulse begin to race and my breathing become laboured, with each step increasing the anxiety I felt all through my body. When I turned to Ryokan and told him that I could not go any further, he agreed that we should leave it to another time.

Despite many further attempts at Zen walking in that direction through the woods, the same heightened levels of anxiety prevented me from going any further. Eventually even Ryokan agreed that this was causing me more harm than good, and it was discontinued.

Over thirty years later, despite all my advances in Zen meditation, whatever that traumatic experience was remains blocked from my memory. And now today, as I follow the policeman through the woods, with each step I take that old anxiety within me grows stronger. I realise that the source of my anxiety is in this walking through the woods toward something traumatic that I would rather not confront.

'Not far now, sir,' the policeman says. 'Just beyond those trees.'

I force myself to continue, dreading to think what I might have to look at. And then, through the trees, I see an old wooden hut covered in snow, with another policeman standing at the door.

As we draw close, the policeman salutes Inspector Kaneko and stands aside to let us enter. The evening sunset through one small window falls on Ame's pitifully small body, still curled up in the corner where he was found. He looks like he has simply fallen asleep.

'I'm sorry, sir,' the Inspector says, 'but is that the young man you described?'

'Yes,' I reply quietly. 'That is Ame.'

'I am sorry, sir. Not a very dignified end.'

'No, it isn't,' I reply. 'Have you any idea what may have happened here, Inspector?'

'Hard to say at this stage, sir. Most probably went in his sleep, looking at his position. Probably died of exposure, and ill health by the look of him. We see quite a lot of that with men of the road every winter, I'm afraid. Do you know if he has any family, sir?'

'I'm afraid not, Inspector,' I reply, kneeling down beside him. My feelings of dread now swept away by sheer sorrow, for this tragically sad end to a young man's life.

'What will happen to him now, Inspector?'

'A post mortem, to confirm the cause of death, sir. Then if he has no family, the authorities will see to the cremation.'

'That won't be necessary, Inspector,' I say, touching Ame's cold hand. 'I will look after his funeral.'

'Very well, sir,' the Inspector says. 'If we cannot trace any family, we will let you know when you can make the arrangements. I'll leave you to your privacy for a moment.'

'Thank you, Inspector, that is very kind of you.'

With the Inspector gone, I sit there quietly with Ame. His face looks so serene in death, I believe the Inspector to be right that he must have died peacefully in his sleep. My eyes fall on the broken pot he is still holding to his chest. As I look closer, I see a little red akari inside of it. He must have fallen asleep holding this little makeshift lamp in the night.

And yet, despite the awful sadness before me, the poet within me feels something else. From somewhere, my words come back to me, 'When you see your soul in your haiku, you will have become a haiku master.' There is something in the serene dignity in Ame's face in repose that somehow makes me think that he may have actually achieved this goal at the end.

'Are you alright, sir?' the Inspector asks me yet again as I emerge from the hut.'

'Quite alright now, Inspector,' I reply. 'He is at peace, and I will look after him.'

We drive back in silence, leaving me to watch the sun set behind the trees. The haiku master Shoson said that in a haiku moment, the poet intuitively glimpses some profound essence of the experience of life. I have no way to describe why, but I have a real sense that Ame may have had such an experience in that solitary place before he died.

Within the haiku tradition, poets attempt to compose one final haiku before dying, to try and express the essence of their art. Sadly no one will ever know if Ame achieved this, but my poet's intuition tells me that he did. And then I am reminded of the hauntingly beautiful words of the haiku master Takeo about the death of someone who was very dear to him.

Talking stops
white petals
falling in my heart.

As we drive back through the village, I ask the Inspector to drop me off at the harbour, as I don't feel quite ready to go home just yet.

'Are you sure you will be alright here, sir?' he asks as I get out.

'I'll be fine, Inspector,' I assure him. 'But just one thing before you go. When I saw Ame last, he told me of his plans to return home, an old boathouse, as I recall. He was heading north, because we talked about his travels all around the coast.'

'Thank you, sir,' the Inspector says, making a note of it in his book. 'That does give me something to go on. O-yasumi nasai sir.'

I wish him goodnight in return, then watch as he drives off into the night until the car's red taillights fade into the darkness. I turn and look at the harbour. The fishing boats have all returned and are tied up for the night. I take a slow walk past them with my thoughts on Ame.

Once again, Uko's haiku about the nightingale singing in the echo of the bell tolled at evening comes to mind. There is a feeling of peace here in the harbour, with the boats at rest for the night. I think of the Shinto ceremony we hold every year for those lost at sea, to pray that their souls are now at rest in that place beyond the sea. It feels fitting that I say my prayer for Ame here, as I remember our first meeting by the shore of the sea, when he showed me his haiku about the pebbles on the beach waiting for the waves.

When I finally make my way up the hill and retire for the night, I lay awake watching the moon with its almost human face looking down upon the earth with an expression of compassion. And then the moon is obscured by huge snowflakes gently falling to earth. Before I surrender to sleep, I compose one final haiku for the young homeless poet.

Snow falling softly
in white silence
as the poet sleeps.

5

The wild geese take flight
low along the railroad tracks
in the moonlit night.
Shiki

Inspector Keneko returned a few days later to inform me that the post mortem had confirmed his suspicion that Ame had died of a combination of exposure and ill health from sleeping rough for so long. Therefore, if I still wished, I could arrange his funeral.

As he appeared to have no surviving family, the Inspector left Ame's few possessions with me: the broken pot with the akari inside it, which he had been holding to his chest when he died, and his collection of haiku, written upon old scraps of rice paper found in the pockets of his old coat, which Inspector Keneko had tactfully decided not to bring, as it was in too poor a condition.

As I looked through his haiku, my own one about the leaves in the stream stood out only because it was the only one on a proper piece of good quality paper. And that, to my mind was the only difference in quality, because his haiku are at least the equal of mine if not even better.

His haiku are stunning in their vibrancy, all about his travels all around Japan. There is a fragrance of freshness running through them, as though seeing the world for the first time. And yet, beneath this freshness there flows a deep sense of the makato, the mystery beneath the beauty, lying just beyond the words of his haiku, enticing the reader to take a step beyond that veil that separates the shasei from the makato, the physical from the transcendent.

When Ame first showed me his haiku of the white wings of swans flying into the clouds, I was struck by its simplicity and freshness. But as I read it again in context with all his other haiku, I found the depth of the makato striking and the equal of even Shiki's classic haiku about wild geese flying low along railroad tracks in moonlight. The tragedy here is not only that this young poet died so young, but also that this vibrant talent for haiku has been lost to the world.

My plan is to put all of Ame's haiku into a volume and have it published, with a foreword written by me about this young poet's Japanese odyssey and the haiku that it produced. When he asked me how he could become a haiku master, I had told him that only haiku could teach him how to become a master. It is now clear to me that he achieved his goal, for there is a freshness and clarity here that is of the essence of haiku. I was therefore right not to try to give him any advice, which might only have clouded his vision and dulled the vibrancy of his work. When confronted by such natural talent as this, the wise haiku teacher knows when to remain silent.

Ame's funeral service was very simple. Perhaps, as a haiku poet, he would have liked it that way. My Zen friend Ryokan accompanied me to the cremation service. Afterwards we spent some time at my home in the garden where I had planned to lay Ame's ashes to rest. It seemed a fitting place, as it was here that Ame and I had stood on the bridge looking at the fallen leaves drifting away in the stream.

However, my plans for Ame's ashes changed when Inspector Kaneko turned up again at my house the following day. He informed me that going on my information about Ame going north along the coast to get to his old boathouse, he had actually discovered his village, which was only a few miles north of where his body was found. The Inspector said that after making inquiries, he found out that Ame had been Christian and that he had contacted the local priest on my behalf, a Fr. Koji, who would be happy to have a memorial service for him.

And so today I am setting off to catch the coast bus to take Ame home to his own village. I find it very poignant that Ame failed to complete his Japanese odyssey all the way around the coast back to his boathouse by only a few short miles. I also feel that it is somehow my duty to take him those last few miles, as he told me that it was actually me who had inspired him to set out to see Fuji-san, although I never for a moment meant for him to walk there. Did this odyssey hasten his death? Possibly, but he was adamant that it had transformed his life completely and helped him to discover his ikigai, his reason for living. While the light of this young life did not burn long, it burned brightly, at least near the end.

It is another fine morning, with winter sunshine and a fresh breeze coming off the sea as I sit by the harbour wall waiting for the bus. When we last talked, Ame was very excited about the prospect of returning home to his old boathouse to live a life of simplicity with his haiku and I have a sense that we are now doing this together, two poets on the last leg of his journey home.

I am possibly more acutely aware than most of the deep-seated longing for the place that is our home. While the people of this village now accept me as one of their own, there remains a part of me that still feels estranged. The only home I have ever known apart from here was of course the monastery, where I was helped so much to begin to build a new life for myself.

The old monastery still holds a very special place in my heart, and it was hard for me to leave that haven of safety. On that morning when I left, I remember tentatively asking Ryokan how one became a Zen monk as I had grown to love the peace that I had found there.

'Not everyone is called to be a Zen monk, Shinjin-san,' he replied gently. 'Nor do they have to, because Zen is within us and all around us.'

151

'And in my case?' I said. 'You believe that the right path for me is now to leave this place.'

'You have made good progress, Shinjin-san,' he replied. 'And it may be that your destiny is to one day become a Zen monk. But for the present I feel that it is time for you to leave, because I feel that if you remained with us, it would be for the wrong reason. One becomes a Zen monk not to escape from the world or from the past, but to embrace reality and the present. But you and I will continue to explore your past, if only to help you let it go and free you to live your life in the present.'

I now feel that Ryokan was right, for I now love my life and realise that I was not destined to become a Zen monk, but I am eternally grateful for his setting me on the path of Zen that has helped me to find my ikigai as a haiku teacher.

There are two aspects of Zen. The first is the himayana, the experience. The second is the makayana, the results of that experience. In some cases, this will indeed lead to a vocation as a Zen monk. In most cases, however, the person will find their ikigai, their reason for living, in other expressions of the Zen way of life, as healers, or teachers, or in my case a simple life as a haiku poet.

When the little coastal bus finally arrives, it is nearly empty and I take a seat at the back on the side of the sea to watch the coast drift by my window. As we head north, we pass through a number of small villages and from my vantage point I can also see some fishing boats further out to sea. Ame's haiku were all about the beauty he saw in this simple yet inspiringly beautiful place. His words enhanced even further by his delicate haikai drawings, to complement the feelings he captured in his haiku.

His love in particular for the place where he was born runs through a lot of his haiku, like a lingering fragrance. The old boathouse appears to encapsulate his love of the life he led there in happier times, and nearer the end drew him like a magnet to return home, like his swans migrating north.

I envy him that feeling, for it is something that has been taken away from me, a sense of where I belong. While I have made a new life for myself in the village where I have lived for over thirty years, there remains this feeling of something missing in my life, something unfulfilled deep within me, that instinct to return to one's place of origin. For me, this is the fragrance running through Shiki's haiku of the geese flying along the railroad tracks in moonlight, the basic instinct to finds one's way back home

Ryokan and I discussed this many times over the years, as our plans failed to let zazen and haiku open up that part of my mind which remains lost. Ryokan now feels that it is unlikely that it will ever return after all this time, and even suggested that perhaps it may be better to remain that way. I was quite upset at this, but he very gently explained that perhaps that traumatic experience, whatever it was, would still be too much for me to face.

From his Zen tradition, Ryokan advised me to try and live simply for the moment, philosophically pointing out that all life in the end is a mystery, Zen in its essence being the acceptance of this and being open to go into the future to let this mystery unfold. Good advice, but as I grow older, this longing to discover who I am keeps returning, like my recurring dream of the boat disappearing over the horizon.

My reflections are now broken as the bus passes the place where Inspector Kaneko stopped the car and we headed up to the place where Ame had been found, and I relive that terrible moment. A few miles further on, the bus driver calls over his shoulder to inform me that this is my stop as the bus pulls into a small fishing village, Ame's home.

One small Japanese fishing village is very like another, and I find this one is very similar to my own, with its small harbour and scattering of boats. I feel quite at home sitting here as I take a moment by the harbour wall, taking in the sea air before I try to find Fr. Koji's church.

It turns out to be quite easy to find, as a local man points it out to me on the top of a hill looking out to sea. It is quite small and simple, sufficient for the few Christian families scattered around these little fishing communities. Catching my breath at the door after my climb up the hill, I take in the view of the sea with the afternoon sun shimmering on the horizon. I can see why Ame loved this place.

Inside, the church is beautifully simple, with white walls and large windows letting in the sunlight, a small crucifix on an alter with snow white linen and a small red akari lamp by the tabernacle. The rest is traditional Japanese in its simplicity, with its polished wooden floor and rows of small wooden satsuru for people to sit on.

The whole place exudes a sense of peace and tranquility, a timelessness and yes, for want of a better word, a holiness that reminds me of my time in the Zen monastery. Then the silence is gently broken by a side door opening as a small man in a brown monk's habit enters. Seeing me, he smiles and comes over.

'Konichiwa,' he says, in a voice just above a whisper, and introduces himself as Fr. Koji. 'And you must be Shijin-san.'

'Konichiwa, father,' I reply. 'I trust that I am not too early.'

'Not at all,' he says, his gentle but very alert eyes turning to my bag. It contains the pot with Ame's ashes, as well as his haiku and of course the old pot with the akari inside it – all he had in the world. 'And I see that you have our young friend Ame with you. Please come through to my house for tea before we have the memorial service.'

I follow Fr. Koji back through the side door to his adjacent house, which turns out to be as small and simple as his church.

'Please take a seat while I prepare some tea,' he says, leaving me to sit by a window overlooking the sea. I smile as I see that his house is almost identical to my own, with its polished wooden floor, a tebaru, satsuru and very little else.

'I trust you had a good journey,' Fr. Koji says, as he brings in the tea and takes a seat.

'A fine drive in the bus along the coast father,' I reply. 'Your village is beautiful.'

'Indeed, it is,' he replies. 'I have had the pleasure of being parish priest here for almost twenty-five years. Doesn't time fly?'

'Quicker with every passing year father.' I feel myself warming to this old priest, whose relaxed and gentle manner puts me at my ease.

'Just so, just so,' he says, pouring the tea. 'Now you must tell me something about yourself, Shijin-san, and how you came to know our young friend Ame.'

By the time we had finished our tea, this gentle unassuming old priest has quietly and skillfully found out almost everything about me, my love of haiku and how it brought Ame and I together.

'And no memory at all of your life before this friend of yours found you at his monastery door, Shinjin-san? How very difficult for you. But how fortunate in your finding your way to the Zen monk's door. God works in mysterious ways, does he not?'

'And Ame, father?' I say trying to turn the conversation away from me. 'I was hoping that you might be able to tell me something of his life here before he took to the road.'

'A sad case, Shijin-san,' the priest said, turning his gaze out to sea. 'A very sad case indeed. I baptised him, you know, as an infant. His mother, Taki-san – a lovely person – had him out of wedlock when her fiancé was lost at sea. Taki-san herself lost both her parents as an infant. I never met them, both died before I took up residence here as parish priest.'

The old priest paused for a moment, with his gaze turning once again out to sea, as though reflecting upon what he should tell me next.

'I was told that her mother died in childbirth,' he continued. 'And that her father, poor man in his grief, walked into the sea. His body was never found. Taki-san lived for her son and was devoted to him, but on her death, he was left destitute and physically unable to fend for himself. The rest you know, he took to the road as a beggar. And now you have brought him home, Shijin-san.'

'I trust we can find a suitable place of rest for him here, father.'

'Oh, indeed we can, Shijin-san,' the priest said. 'Indeed, we can. But first let us take him back into the church to entrust his soul to God.'

6

Footprints in the sand
haiku on fragile paper
fading memories.
Shijin.

Ame's memorial service was beautifully simple in the church where the old priest had baptised him as an infant in his mother's arms. There is now a sense of things being put right for him. The passing of his young life treated with the dignity that it deserves.

'And now, Shijin-san,' Fr. Koji says. 'We must take our young friend and lay him to rest.'

With Fr. Koji now wrapped in a heavy mantle over his habit, we leave the church behind us and make our way down the hill and through the village, heading toward Ame's boathouse. And then, on the edge of the village, I see it: a rather ramshackle old place right on the water's edge. Even from a distance, one can tell that it has seen better days and is quite neglected. An old boat lies tethered to the porch, and I can picture Ame here in happier times, sitting by the boat, looking out to sea and drawing his swans.

But then, for some strange reason, as I drew near to the old place, I begin to experience that same sense of uneasiness that I felt when I approached the old hut where Ame died.

'Are you alright?' Fr. Koji asks, as I slow my pace.

'I'm fine,' I reply. 'Just slowing down a bit with age.'

Fr. Koji smiles and we continue on at a slower pace, as my uneasiness continues to grow. Then, as we step onto the old jetty and walk toward the door, I feel that sense of anxiety begin to escalate, the old fear rising up again of walking through the woods toward something I sense is going to be traumatic. But there are no trees here, only ocean; it does not make any sense.

'Are you quite sure that you are alright?' Fr. Koji asks again. 'For you have turned quite pale. If this is too much for you, we can come back another day.'

'I'm fine, father,' I lie. 'Just a little short of breath.'

'If you're sure,' the priest says, looking unconvinced as he opens the door of the old boathouse.

'So, this is where he lived,' I say, more to myself than to the priest.

'Indeed,' Fr. Koji replies. 'This was their home.'

The old oak floor creaks in protest against our weight as we cross the threshold. In that moment, I have the distinct feeling that I have been here before. I have to rest my hand upon the door for a second to steady myself, as Fr.Koji leads the way.

'Taki-san never did get round to fixing that creaking board,' the priest says. 'But whenever I visited them here, the love in this old place was everywhere I looked. She was totally devoted to her son, you know. Probably worked herself to an early death making enough to keep this old roof over their head.'

With my eyes adjusting to the faint light of the winter sun drifting in through the window, I begin to see those little signs of love all around the old place. Their tatami rolled up and placed neatly against the wall. A few little pieces of traditional haikai art, most probably Ame's, placed into frames. A little photograph of a painting of a kintsukuroi pot placed by a small tebaru, to catch the sunlight through the window.

'They were happy here, father.'

'Oh yes, Shijin-san. Desperately poor, but happy none the less. And possibly even more so, because they knew what really mattered, having each other. She was a beautiful haiku poet, you know.'

'No, I did not know that, father. Ame never said. We only spoke about his haiku on the two brief occasions that we met.'

'And, I in turn, did not know that Ame wrote haiku,' says the old priest.

'Perhaps you might like to look at his haiku,' I say, taking them out of my bag and putting them on the tebaru.

As I do so, Fr. Koji's eyes fall on the broken pot with the red akari still inside it.

'Good heavens,' the old priest says, picking up the akari. 'I gave that to Taki-san when she brought him to be baptised. And he has carried that with him in all his travels?'

'He died with it in his arms, father,' I reply.

The old priest just shakes his head in silent wonder, then very tenderly replaces the akari back in the old pot.

'And these are his haiku,' he says, picking up the little ragged pile of rice papers and looking through them very slowly and respectfully.

'But these are quite delightful, Shijin-san,' he says. 'And I believe that I can detect his mother's influence here. She was completely untrained, you know, a totally natural talent.'

'As was Ame,' I reply. 'And possibly all the better for that. In my opinion, his work is worthy of publishing and I intend to see to it.'

'How fitting,' the old priest says, tenderly leafing through the rest of the haiku.

'What will happen to this old place now, father?' I ask. The thought of all these little personal reminders of their life here being lost, yet another poignant twist of their fate.

'With no surviving relatives, I suppose the authorities will sell it off for what they can get for it. So sad to see the old place which they loved fall into other hands. But perhaps we should now be getting on, Shijin-san, while the daylight is still with us. We have a good half hour sail each

159

way, and I'm not as young as I used to be. And what about you, ever done any sailing?'

'My friend Ryokan found me a job helping out on a fishing boat when I left the monastery. But before that, I have no idea.'

'Of course. How tactless of me, your amnesia. Well, we will do our best, Shijin-san. And I must confess that since Ame left, I have taken it upon myself to keep an eye on the old place, in the hope of his return. I took the liberty of taking the old boat out a few times when the weather was fine.'

Fr. Koji closes the door very respectfully as we leave, pausing a little as he does so, which I suspect is to say a silent prayer for Ame and his mother.

'Now then, Shinjin-san,' he says, stepping carefully into the old boat. 'If you would kindly untie the rope then step aboard, we will get under way.'

For an elderly priest, his handling of the old boat is quite impressive, and I detect a wiry strength within that small frame beneath his big heavy mantle.

'How many years have you been a priest, Fr. Koji?' I ask politely.

'I entered the Franciscan order quite late when I was almost thirty,' he replies.

'So, you did not always feel the call to the priesthood then?'

'Quite so. I tried a number of things, as one does when one is young, but found them all somehow lacking. I found myself searching for something deeper. Eventually I found my way to the order of St. Francis, attracted by the saint's mystical spirituality. He saw the world as a holy place, touched by God when he walked by the shore, spoke to the wind and calmed the sea. That reverence for nature remains very much part of my spirituality, especially here in this beautiful coastline. I believe that we all have our own spiritual path to follow, don't you, Shijin-san?'

'I do indeed, father.'

'And yourself, Shijin-san? Are you a man of faith? You mentioned your friend being a Zen monk.'

'I like to think that I have an open mind on the subject, father. But I do practice Zen meditation. I suppose my haiku are the nearest thing I have to a religion.'

'A window into the mystery that surrounds us?' suggests the old priest, fixing his eye upon me.

'Quite so, father,' I reply, using one of the old priest's expressions, which brings a smile to his face.

We let the conversation drop as Fr. Koji takes the boat out into deep water, the old boat beginning to rise and fall with the waves as the priest tacks across the wind to fill the sail. From my position in the bow of the boat, I look over the old priest's shoulder watching the boathouse shrink away in the distance.

'If you look to the front, you will soon be able to see our destination,' Fr. Koji says after a while.

Turning around, I catch sight of two large outcrops of rock jutting out of the sea. Then, as we pull alongside, I notice the large Shinto rope binding the rocks together.

'Ame asked me to lay Taki-san's ashes to rest here,' the old priest explained. 'It was their special place to remember Ame's father, who was lost at sea. I know that he would have wanted me to do the same for him.'

'A beautiful end to a tragic young life, father,' I suggest.

'Or a tragically beautiful young life,' Fr. Koji says, and I bow my head in reply. The old priest certainly has a way with words.

'Tie the rope off please, Shijin-san,' he says as he pulls down the sail. We sit there in silence for a moment, with the boat secured to the big Shinto rope, listening to the waves lapping between the boat and the rocks.

The old priest then takes out the small prayer shawl which he had worn for Ame's memorial back at the church and wraps it around his shoulders.

'If you would hold the urn of Ame's ashes, Shijin-san, we will proceed,' he says.

His prayers for the soul of Ame to rest in peace are beautifully simple, as is the manner in which the old priest says them, in a quiet and dignified way. It is of course sheer coincidence, but at that point the wind dies down and a silence descends upon our little ceremony.

After a silent pause, Fr. Koji invites me to simply put the little pot gently into the sea then let it sink down into the deep. Then we both sit there for a moment with our own silent reflections about the young life we had paid our final respects to.

'Domo origato, Fr. Koji,' I say, bowing formally. 'That was beautifully done.'

'He is at peace,' the old priest says. 'And with his mother. And I feel that there is something very right about this, Shinjin-san, something of a synchronicity.'

'Synchronicity, father?'

'Events occurring in time and place that seem somehow very fitting, and beyond mere chance,' the old priest replies. 'Take yourself, for instance. A chance meeting with Ame results in his setting off on an odyssey all around Japan, then another chance meeting with you on his return, which eventually results in you bringing him home to be placed at rest with his mother. Random coincidence? Or something deeper at work?'

With this question left hanging in the air unanswered, we untie the line from the Shinto rope and push the boat away from the rocks with the oars. Then Fr. Koji hoists the sail and we head back to the boathouse.

7

Jewels of the sea
polished smooth by time and tide
washed into the deep.
Shijin

We speak little on the return sail, each of us engaged in our own thoughts, until Fr. Koji brings the boat back alongside the jetty and I make it secure with the rope.

'Will you come back to the house for something to eat?' Fr. Koji asks, as we step back onto the jetty and take a moment to look back out to sea.

'Thank you, father,' I reply, 'but I think I will stay here a little longer.'

'I understand,' he says. 'And now I feel that I must thank you, for everything you have done for our young friend.' Then, out of the blue, he does something quite extraordinary and puts his hand very gently on my head.

'God bless,' he says, in such a natural and sincere way that robs the gesture of any sense of offence.

'Do you mind if I ask you something, father?'

'Not at all,' he replies.

'It's just that you seem very much at peace, even at ease within yourself, and yet you must have to do this type of thing so often. Does all this sadness never cause you to doubt what you believe?'

The old priest is silent for a long moment as he holds my gaze with those gentle but very deep eyes. Eyes that had seen more than his share of the joys and sorrows of this world.

'We are stardust, Shijin-san,' he says finally. 'Our world and everything within it, created from the dust of countless exploding stars within an infinite universe. The ultimate question therefore is this: Is it all random coincidence? Or is there, as I believe, a divine force behind this mystery, guiding us toward our destiny? And that is why I became a priest. Sayonara, Shijin-san,' he says with a smile. 'I will leave you to decide.'

'Sayonara, Fr. Koji,' I reply. 'It was a pleasure to meet you. And you have given me much to think about.'

'Quite so, Shijin-san, quite so,' he replies. 'And remember what the haiku master Buson said. "In a haiku moment the poet catches a fleeting glimpse of the makato, the mysterious reality beneath the surface of the shasai."'

I watch him take his leave back along the jetty, with his question on the mystery of life hanging in the space between us. An interesting man, this Fr. Koji, leaving me with more questions than answers.

I still have an hour or so before I have to catch the last coast bus home, so I make my way back into the boathouse to rest with my thoughts. As I go through the door, that sense of déjà vu is even stronger now that I am left on my own within this old place. I try to shake it off, telling myself that it is just an old, deserted house. But there remains an unshakable sense that I have been here before.

With the setting sun shining through the window, I sit down at the tebaru and begin to look through Ame's collection of haiku and haikai drawings, imagining him in this old place which he loved so much. His drawings capture the feel of this old place perfectly. As I read his haiku I lose all sense of time, following his travels all through Japan.

It is only when I begin to find it difficult to read the words that I realise that the sun has almost set. Reaching into my bag of Ame's possessions, I take out his akari and light it. With his own light shining upon his haiku, I become very aware that this was his home, the place he loved so dearly.

I continue reading through his haiku until I notice that the sky outside the window has gone from sunset red to indigo blue, and that I have completely lost track of the time. The last bus will by now have gone and I have no other means to get home.

I feel that it would be too much of an imposition to call upon Fr Koji to ask him to put me up for the night. So, with no other option, I resign myself to having to spend the night here in the old boathouse and catch the first bus home again in the morning.

Having lain empty for so long, with the coming of night I become more aware of the sense of cold and dampness in the old place and set about trying to light a fire in the old stove with the bits of driftwood laying piled up beside it. With a bit of effort, I manage to get it going and with that and Ame's akari light, the old place begins to feel a bit more hospitable.

As I continue to read through Ame's haiku, I come to the one which he wrote that day when we met on the beach, about the pebbles waiting for the tide. I turn it over and smile as I see the haiku that I wrote for him on the reverse:

> Jewels of the sea
> polished smooth by time and tide
> washed into the deep.

Two haiku, one piece of rice paper, one moment in time. And then, without any conscious thought on my part, I slide my hand over the drawer of the tebaru, feeling the smoothness of the polished wood. And as I do so the drawer moves very slightly. It is of course an intrusion of privacy, but I open the drawer to find a beautiful little brown book with a golden butterfly etched onto the edges of the pages.

Fascinated by this motif, I thumb the pages into a fan and watch the butterfly as it appears to fly. The whole effect is delightful. Once again, I cannot resist yet another intrusion of privacy and I open the book to find that it contains a collection of beautifully written haiku, all signed by Taki, Ame's mother.

Old Fr. Koji had described her as being a beautiful person, and that sentiment is echoed on every page of this little book of the most exquisite haiku. It is like finding the secret source from which Ame's natural talent flowed, and from a girl called Taki, waterfall.

By the time I turn the last page of Taki's book of haiku, I feel that I have been given a private insight into this beautiful person's life. I can almost see her sailing her boat in this lovely bay, walking along the beach with her son, sitting by their fire in the evening. Her very last entry in the book is a very atmospheric little haiku about hearing Ame's swans calling to each other like voices through the mist out in the bay, which of course must have been the last haiku she ever wrote.

The final haiku of a poet is held in reverence as the ultimate expression of their art, their parting gift to the world after a lifetime of capturing the essence of those transiently beautiful haiku moments for others to experience. The haiku master Shoson put it quite beautifully, saying that in a haiku moment the poet may glimpse something of the essence of life. This can be particularly true near the end of their life. It is said that the seventeen syllables within the three lines of a haiku should be read in one breath, like a sigh as one who experiences something that is amari-ni-utsukushi, too beautiful for this world. And I feel that there is a fragrance of that in Taki-san's last haiku.

I place the book still open with a sense of reverence next to Ame's collection of haiku. Two poets, side by side in their haiku. Sitting here in the silence of the night, with the little akari casting its warm light on their haiku, I remember how I found it held to his chest within the little broken pot. And so, in memory of him, I take out the broken pot, put the akari inside it and watch as streams of light shine out through all the cracks in the pot, filling the old boathouse with its fragile light. It strikes me as very poignant, that this is most likely the last thing that Ame looked at in that old hut before he died.

I hear Fr. Koji's parting words echo in my mind. 'In a haiku moment the poet glimpses something of the mystery that lies hidden beneath the shasai.' It is as though Ame has left this little silent haiku for me to discover its mystery. I feel that there is indeed something here, something in the way in which the streams of light fall onto the haiku. Something just below the surface of my mind, just beyond my grasp. Like the voices of Taki's swans echoing through the mist, the sound just too far off for me to hear what it is they are calling. Try as I might, the mystery eludes me until finally I give in to my feelings of tiredness. It has been an emotionally exhausting day, and I now feel the need to try and get some sleep.

I unroll one their tatami and lay down by the window. For a winter's night it is surprisingly mild outside, and I leave the window open to listen to the sea. The stove in the corner continues to give a sense of comfort to the old place as the embers of the driftwood crackle and burn slowly down. Ame's akari within the old broken pot looks as though it has another hour or two left, so I just leave it to burn itself out.

As I feel my eyes begin to grow heavy with sleep, I have a sense of contentment in that I have now done all that I can for the young poet whom I met so briefly, but who had such a profound influence upon me. There is a sense that things have been put right by him now, with Fr. Koji's words echoing once again, 'He is at peace, and with his mother.'

With these thoughts drifting through my mind, I feel sleep begin to overtake me. Listening to the crackling of the driftwood in the stove... listening to the waves outside... listening to the water lapping against the old boat tied to the jetty... listening...

And now I am standing outside the boathouse in the moonlight, listening to the waves, looking up into a night sky full of stars. Stepping into the boat, I untie the rope and push away from the jetty, letting the boat glide away upon an ocean of midnight blue.

I unfurl the sail and sit down in the stern as the wind fills the sail and I turn the rudder to bring the boat around to head north along the coast. I have no fear of the sea, and I know exactly where I am going, for I have sailed there many times before.

I bring the sail about and turn into shore, letting the boat come to ground in the soft sand. Then I step over the sand and make my way up the beach toward the little waterfall that glistens in the moonlight like a cascade of stars.

My lovely wife is waiting for me here, in this our very special place, holding our newborn daughter out for me to take her in my arms. 'Her name is Taki-san,' she says. But as I kiss our little waterfall, her face is so very cold. And as I give her back to my wife, her face is now also very cold. The coldness reaches into my mind with its icy fingers, too unbearable, and my mind turns black.

I awake with a cold wind blowing in through the window, stunned as I lay in the dark, staring into the night. My mind struggles to cope with what I have seen in my dream, the truth hidden in this old boathouse. The truth now revealed in my dream. The truth of who I am. The truth of that terrible thing which my mind shut down to erase from my memory. The truth that I am Taki-san's father. She is the daughter I thought had died in childbirth with my wife. And this old boathouse is my home.

8

Following a storm
fishing boats on still waters
quiet reflections.
Shijin

With the moon shining through the window, I watch the last flickers of flame die out within Ame's akari, the light that my young grandson held in his arms as he died alone in that old hut, but the light that reached out to me and united me with the family that I never knew I had. Three haiku poets finally brought together through their words. Some day I will perhaps be able to capture this moment in haiku, but not yet, for this moment is beyond words.

In the silence of the night, I let my eyes roam around the boathouse, my home, now bathed in moonlight. Then my eyes come to rest upon Taki-san's book of haiku, lying where I left it on the tebaru at which she sat to write them. I feel strangely close to her at this moment, almost as though she had left these very personal poems for me to read.

I search around for another candle and light it within the akari. Then I sit down to read my daughter's book of haiku all over again. It is like a little window into the life of the daughter I had never known, and every page touches my heart and draws me a little closer to this very beautiful poet. When I finally close the last page of her book, I am determined that these words so dear to her heart will not be lost. My daughter's haiku will be included with my grandson's as a lasting memorial to their memory. I was not there to help her through her life, but at least now, as her father, I can help her life to be remembered.

In a moment of inspiration, as is often the case with poets, I realise that Ame and Taki's book of haiku would not be complete without my own. Three poets, three leaves in a stream of time, three ripples in the sea, converging to create their unique story. Not simply a book of our haiku, but a book of the story through which our haiku finally brought us together.

When the sun comes up in the morning, I am still sitting at Taki-san's tebaru, as I had found it impossible to sleep after the events which had unfolded in the night. Getting stiffly to my feet, I step out onto the jetty and into the old boat. As I sit in the stern, I run my hand over the haiku which I had carved there, on that that terrible day when my wife Mariko-san died, and I see my name, Kyoshi, carved their into the wood of this old boat which I sailed in this beautiful bay. I sit here in the boat for a very long time, remembering my fishing trips so many years ago with Mariko-san waiting on the jetty to welcome me home.

Then I know what I must do to bring Mariko-san back to me. I unfurl the sail and cast off the old rope from the jetty, then take our old boat out to sea. With the fresh sea breeze in my face, I turned the boat north on a heading toward our very special place, the little cove with the waterfall.

The boat responds beautifully to my touch, riding the waves easily, built by a master craftsman with every beam molded to perfection to glide through the water. Following my dream, I bring the boat into the cove, taking her right up onto the sand. Then I make my way slowly up to the little waterfall and sit there with all my lost memories flowing back to me.

This was our special place. Sometimes Mariko-san and I would spend the whole night here sleeping under the stars. As I sit here, I can almost hear her voice calling to me through the falling water, telling me once again that our beautiful daughter's name is Taki-san. Of course, it had to be, because it was here on one of our moonlit nights under the stars that we created her.

With tears of joy and of sadness running down my face, I feel once again that terrible pain, like a knife piercing my heart when Mariko-san died. I experienced a pain and a sorrow that my mind could hardly endure. For Mariko-san had been my life, the wind in my sail and the breath in my body, how could I go on living? And then I looked down to see that my daughter had also stopped breathing, and my mind had shut down into blackness.

I tell Mariko-san how our beautiful daughter has reached out to me with her haiku and touched my mind and my heart with her healing words. And that I have seen her, seen her in the face of Ame, her son, the haiku poet whose words led me back to this place which was lost to me for so long. This place which I shall never leave again.

While I have grown to love my little house at the top of the hill overlooking the harbour, it is the boathouse that is my home and a part of who I am. It is filled with treasured memories of the things I did and the people who lived there, who were lost to me, and now I have them all back again.

I reach out and gently touch the waterfall, as though touching Mariko-san's hand, until I come again to sit beside her in this our special place. Then I get back into our old boat and sail her back to the boathouse. In the cold light of day, the old place has clearly seen better days and is looking rather ramshackle, but I feel that it is part of its charm. Life is beautiful here on the Hokkaido coast, not because it is perfect but because it is fragile and vulnerable with the passing of the years, just like Ame's old broken pot.

I tie up the boat and make my way back into the boathouse. Sitting down at Taki-san's tebaru, I let my eyes drift up to the picture of the kintsukuroi on the wall. Its fragile beauty is enhanced by the threads of molten gold holding the broken pieces together, like our broken lives that need to be held together by love.

And so, as I sit here in the old boathouse, I pause to reflect upon an appropriate title for our book. The book of our words which reached out to join us together in that love which we shared for haiku. Pebbles on a beach, perhaps? Or perhaps leaves flowing in a stream? I smile as I realise that there is only one title that can hold our three lives together as one. Picking up Taki-san's pen, I write the title of our book.

The Boathouse.

THE END

BROKEN POTS: INTRODUCTION

The inspiration for *The Boathouse* grew out of the 'Broken Pots' poem, just as the poem grew out of the old broken pot which I found in the garden of the hospice where I work.

The broken pot seemed to encapsulate all the unanswerable questions about the brokenness that most of us feel at some point in our lives. And so, I took it back into the hospice with me and gave it a place by the window of our quiet room, where people come to try and find a sense of peace within their brokenness.

That was two years ago, and over that time, the little broken pot has continued to speak to many other people, in its own silent way, as the light from the candle radiates out of all its cracks and crevices. A light shining in the darkness, a symbol of healing in our fragility.

And so, eventually I wrote a poem about the little pot. I have lost count of the number of people who have told me just how much the poem and the broken pot have meant to them. Over five hundred copies have now gone from the quiet room, with people telling me that they have sent them to loved ones all over the world. All from a little broken pot lying in a garden.

The last verse of the poem speaks about the secrets that lie hidden all around us, under every leaf and rock and old broken pot. Like the secret beauty hidden within every human soul. The little broken pot had however another secret waiting for me to find, the secret of my first novel *The Boathouse*, which is all about finding our secret inner beauty and our reason for living.

Broken Pots.

Behind the Garden House Hospice there's a little wooden shed where I go to sit when I feel the need for a moment of a quiet reflection. Around the door of the shed there is a collection of old earthenware pots, all shapes and sizes, and all with their own unique characteristics and little imperfections, just like us. At my feet lies a little broken pot that has been cast aside, too badly broken to be of any use. Sitting here with the little broken pot growing warm in my hands, I think of all the broken people who have held my hand and asked me why? Why has this happened to me? I don't know why, no-one knows why. But the little broken pot in my hands seems to tell me, in its own silent way, that we are all broken, one way or another. And that in some mysterious way this brokenness somehow makes us even more human, in our vulnerability and need for care and compassion.

When my moment of quiet reflection is over, I carry the little broken pot back into the hospice with me and place it on the window of our quiet room, where people come to find some sense of peace among all their brokenness. Before I go off duty, I look in on my little pot, now bathed in moonlight casting silvery blue shadows on the window. I notice that someone has lit a little candle and placed it beside my broken pot. Perhaps the little pot has spoken, in its own silent way, to someone else's heart. The candle seems to highlight all the little pots imperfections, casting deep shadows among all the broken bits. But when I put the candle inside the little pot, its inner beauty is revealed as the light streams out through every crack and crevice, transforming it into a work of art? Or a symbol of light shining in the darkness? Or perhaps even a symbol of inner healing. Because the little pot doesn't look broken any more, and its fragility only seems to deepen its sense of translucent beauty.

The thing about symbols is that they can speak to us in a way that transcends words. Sitting here in the moonlight with the little broken pot glowing warmly in my hands, it speaks to me once again, in its own silent way. It tells me that we don't have to be afraid of being broken, or try to hide it by pretending to be perfect, because no-one is perfect. And that its through our brokenness that we become more sensitive to the brokenness of others and more open to give and to receive care and compassion. It is then that our hidden human beauty is most truly revealed, precisely through our fragility and brokenness.

The little broken pot now lives permanently on the window of the hospice quiet room with a little light burning day and night inside it. It still speaks to many people in its own silent way. I sometimes wonder if the little broken pot and I were destined to meet, like soul mates. There is an American Indian prayer which asks God for the wisdom to understand the secret which he has hidden under every leaf and rock. The secret which I found hidden in the little broken pot is that there is an eternal beauty hidden within every human soul that can sometimes only be seen when we are at our most vulnerable and fragile. It is then that the light shines out through all our brokenness to make us whole again.

Doug Murray ©

174

Comments on The Boathouse

This is a delicate, contemplative novel comprised of three characters and the boathouse that links them together in a meditative form of prose.

The book has a distinctive tone of peace that suits the story perfectly. A real joy and escape for those who read it.

The three-part structure is unique and fits the unique style of writing and the three protagonists nicely.

This book is poetic in style, the descriptive delicate style of writing is particularly fitting given that one of the book's themes is haiku.

The descriptions of Japan and the culture woven into the novel give you a vivid feel of being elsewhere, a novel that presents a country to you as well as a story.

Made in the USA
Las Vegas, NV
09 January 2025

16129049R00098